The Runaway

A Maryellen Mystery

by Alison Hart

✳ American Girl®

Special thanks to Judy Woodburn

Published by American Girl Publishing

17 18 19 20 21 22 LEO 11 10 9 8 7 6 5 4 3 2 1

Cover image by Juliana Kolesova and Michael Dwornik

The following individuals and organizations have given permission to
use images incorporated into the cover design: iStock.com/DorianGray
(telephone pole sign); iStock.com/HighLaZ (dogs in cage); iStock.com/
MivPiv (ice cream truck); iStock.com/marchello74 (neighborhood); iStock.
com/Frizzantine (body with crossed arms).

Cataloging-in-Publication Data available from the Library of Congress.

americangirl.com/service

Beforever™

The adventurous characters you'll meet in
the BeForever books will spark your curiosity
about the past, inspire you to find your voice
in the present, and excite you about your future.
You'll make friends with these girls as you share
their fun and their challenges. Like you, they are
bright and brave, imaginative and energetic,
creative and kind. Just as you are, they are
discovering what really matters: Helping others.
Being a true friend. Protecting the earth.
Standing up for what's right. Read their stories,
explore their worlds, join their adventures.
Your friendship with them will BeForever.

TABLE *of* CONTENTS

chapter 1
Scooter

"FETCH, SCOOTER!" MARYELLEN
Larkin tossed a chewed tennis ball across the front
lawn. Scooter, the Larkin family's aging dachshund,
sat down on the grass and rolled over onto his back.
"I mean, roll over," Maryellen quickly said, snapping
a rope in the air as if she were a lion tamer at the circus. Scooter yawned and wiggled his pudgy paws.

Maryellen rolled her eyes and then bowed to a
pretend audience. "And that, ladies and gentlemen, is
the fierce Leo, the African circus lion, waving *adieu.*"

Dropping the rope, she flopped on the ground
beside Scooter. "You are so talented—as long as I give
the command *after* you've done something," she said
with a chuckle. Maryellen loved to act out exciting
scenes in which Scooter usually played an important

1

role. He'd been rescued from pretend danger count-less times, and even lassoed by the Lone Ranger (played by Maryellen). He'd been Thunderbolt, the wonder horse, and Sea Wolf, the pirate's companion. Maryellen counted Scooter as one of her best friends.

Smiling up at the clouds, she scratched the dog's stomach. It was a chilly January afternoon in Daytona Beach, and a stiff breeze ruffled the broad leaves of the palm trees on her street, but the sun was warm. Scooter loved tummy scratches, and he sighed and waved his paws again, this time at a man in a uniform striding down the sidewalk.

Maryellen popped up. "Hello, Mr. Beamer. Any mail?"

"Yes sirreee!" The postman held up a handful of envelopes. "And I believe there's one in the stack you've been waiting for."

Maryellen jumped to her feet. "Oooh—one of our contest entries?"

"Might be." He handed her the envelopes.

She quickly leafed through them. *Whoo-wee*—
one was from General Mills, the cereal company!
Maryellen's heart beat a little faster. She and her mom
had been entering contests for weeks. She was especially proud of one cereal jingle they'd thought up:
"Kids eat Wheaties for a breakfast treatie!"

At first, she and her mother had entered one
contest for fun. They'd enjoyed thinking up clever
rhymes for the product so much that they'd entered
as many contests as they could find. "This is exercise
for my brain," Mrs. Larkin had said laughingly. The
prizes were pretty exciting, too, even if they hadn't
won anything yet.

Some of the contests, like "Win a Schwinn!," were
advertised in magazines. Others, like "Win a trip
to New York" on Scooter's bag of Chow-Chow Dog
Food, had directions and forms on the back of the
product. To enter the Wheaties contest, Mrs. Larkin
had bought boxes and boxes of the cereal and cut
out the entry blanks, which they'd sent in with their

jingles. Maryellen thought it was pretty smart for the companies to hold the contests, because people had to buy more products just to get the entry forms. She had forgotten how many contests they'd entered, but she was sure that this time they had won.

"Thank you, Mr. Beamer! Come on, Scooter." She dashed onto the front steps and held open the screen door. The dachshund waddled in ahead of her and plopped on the living room rug near the spot where Beverly, Tom, and Mikey, Maryellen's younger sister and two younger brothers, sat playing Chinese checkers.

"Mom!" Maryellen hollered as the door slammed behind her. "We got a letter from the cereal contest. I think we won!" Waving the envelopes in the air, she ran through the living room, but before she reached the kitchen, her toe caught on a lump. *Oof.* She and the letters went flying.

Her mom stuck her head around the doorway from the kitchen in time to see Maryellen splat on the carpet. A splash of flour dotted Mrs. Larkin's nose. "Are you okay, Ellie?"

Beverly, Tom, and Mikey all giggled when they saw their sister sprawled on the floor. "Mawyellen twipped," Mikey said.

"Over Scooter!" seven-year-old Beverly exclaimed, pointing to the reddish-brown lump that hadn't budged.

"Scooter!" Maryellen scolded as she got up. He woke with a snort and wagged his tail. "Why don't you go outside again? It's nice and sunny." She shooed him out the door and then gathered up the envelopes. "Look, Mom, one is from General Mills!"

"Oooh, do you think we won?" Beverly asked as she jumped to her feet, scattering marbles from the game.

"You mean do you think *Mom and I* won," Maryellen said. "Of course we did—a new freezer!"

"Yippee!" Five-year-old Tom cheered and scratched his elbow at the same time. Both he and

Mikey were getting over the chicken pox. Their faces and arms were splattered with dried spots, and they itched everywhere. "We can fill it with ice cream."

"Let's not get ahead of ourselves." Mrs. Larkin bustled into the living room, wiping her hands on her apron. Gingerly she took the General Mills envelope while Maryellen and her siblings gathered around.

Maryellen held her breath as her mom tore the envelope open, then bounced from foot to foot as her mother pulled out the letter and unfolded it.

"We are happy to inform you that you won . . ." Mrs. Larkin began.

Maryellen leaped in the air like a cheerleader. "We won! We won!" Mikey, Tom, and Beverly danced around echoing her, "We won! We won!"

". . . a year's supply of Wheaties cereal."

Maryellen's cheer died.

Smiling, Mrs. Larkin refolded the letter. "Well, I'm glad you four love Wheaties. We'll be eating it for breakfast, lunch, and dinner." She sighed. "Too bad we didn't win the freezer; it would have been nice to fill with food to feed this big family."

"I love Wheaties," Mikey said solemnly. He was three and the only one not in school yet.

"And they have neato masks on the box that you can cut out," Tom added.

Beverly gave Maryellen a hug. "Don't be sad. You can have the cat mask."

The three went back to their game as if nothing had happened. Maryellen let out a huge sigh; she'd so wanted to win. Not only would the Larkins have gotten a freezer, but her jingle would have been on TV.

She could see herself now—dressed up in her poodle skirt accepting the grand prize. She would scream and cry tears of joy like the winners on television game shows.

"Cheer up, Ellie." Mom chucked her under the chin. "This is the first time we've won anything since we've been entering." Bending, she whispered, "That means we're getting closer to first prize."

"You're right." Maryellen followed her mom into the kitchen. "I'd rather win a new bicycle than a freezer anyway."

Maryellen's bike was a hand-me-down from her oldest sister, Joan, who had handed it down to her next-oldest sister, Carolyn. The handlebars were rusty, the bell didn't ring, and there was no kickstand.

"I know Santa didn't bring you one for Christmas," her mother said, reaching for the tin canister of flour, "but maybe our clever jingle will."

> *Flying fast on your bike,*
> *Windswept green flashing by,*
> *Summer clouds in the sky,*
> *Schwinn Starlet—Queen of the Road!*

Maryellen and her mom sang their jingle together. They'd used the bike's colors in their entry, which was sure to get the judges' attention.

"We should hear from Schwinn any day now," Mrs. Larkin said. "In the meantime, we still have Chow-Chow Dog Food to hear from and more contests to enter." She held up forms they'd cut off the back of Jell-O and Rice Krispies boxes.

"Snap, Crackle, and Slurp!" Maryellen recited. It was only one of several jingles they'd thought up for the cereal.

Her mother laughed. "Keep jingling. I need to finish flouring the chicken. Joan and Jerry are coming for dinner."

Maryellen brightened. Since her sister Joan had gotten married and had started college, the rest of the Larkins didn't see as much of her and her husband, Jerry.

"Will you go tell Carolyn I need her help before she leaves on her date? Then you can set the table."

Maryellen dashed down the hall to the bedroom, where she found her fifteen-year-old sister sitting in front of the mirror. Since Joan had moved out, the girls' room needed only three beds, so now a vanity and a stool with a ruffled skirt filled one corner. Carolyn had decorated the edges of the vanity mirror with photos of movie stars cut from magazines. Maryellen had added a photo of Grandmom and Grandpop, and in the middle, Beverly had taped a paper doll of a princess wearing a tiara.

"Mom needs your help." Maryellen propped her elbows on the vanity and watched as Carolyn brushed on mascara. She was dressed in a pink sweater set with a black scarf tied around her neck, and her blonde hair was wavy. Maryellen thought her sister looked as beautiful as the movie stars in magazines.

"Who's your date tonight?"

"Drew."

Maryellen giggled. "*Dreamy* Drew. Where are you going?" She picked up a tube of lipstick and twisted it.

"Seaside Diner for burgers and shakes," Carolyn replied. "Then they're having the Monday night jukebox dance competition."

"You're going to miss dinner with Joan and Jerry."

"They're meeting us there afterward. The old married couple can still jitterbug like, well, *bugs*. And it won't be late. School tomorrow. But I got all my homework done so Mom said I could go."

"I wish I was old enough to go dancing."

Carolyn took the tube of lipstick and swiped a streak of pink on Maryellen's cheek. "Soon enough, Ellie-bell." Since Joan had left, Carolyn had picked up the habit of rhyming nicknames for her sister. "When you're fifteen like me."

Although Maryellen loved dancing, she couldn't imagine dating, since she was only ten and fifteen was a long ways away. She was best friends with Davy Fenstermacher, who lived next door, and that was A-OK with her.

"Carolyn! Maryellen! I need help, girls!"

"Coming!" they hollered in unison. Maryellen set the table, and Carolyn made biscuits while Mrs. Larkin bathed the itchy boys in powdered oatmeal.

Next, Maryellen frosted the cake for dessert, humming a silly jingle. "Gooey chocolate; covers the city; Superman saves us; because he's so . . . pretty? Gritty? Witty?" Gosh, that jingle would never win anything, she thought, and why wasn't there a Super*girl*?

She tucked a dish towel into her shirt collar as a cape and, twirling around the room, arms outstretched, pretended to fly. A splat of chocolate flew off the knife and landed on the floor. "Hey," Carolyn growled, "don't get any of that on my outfit."

"Sorry." Maryellen quickly wiped up the splatters, and finished the cake with a swirly flourish. "Ta da!"

A honk sounded from outside. Carolyn stuck the biscuits in the oven, called good-bye, and dashed out the front door. Mikey and Tom ran from the bathroom draped only in towels just as Joan and Jerry came in.

At dinner, Mikey and Tom scratched and wiggled, Beverly insisted on sitting on Joan's lap even though she was getting too big, Mr. Larkin advised Jerry about mortgages, and Mrs. Larkin asked Joan about her college classes. Bored, Maryellen plucked a piece of chicken from her drumstick and held it under the table for Scooter, who always waited patiently by her leg for a treat.

When she didn't feel him licking it from her fingers, she bent over and peered under the tablecloth. She saw seven pairs of legs but no dachshund. *That's strange. Scooter always begs during meals. Where is he?*

Maryellen whacked her forehead. Of course! She'd forgotten to give him dinner. He was probably waiting by his food bowl, wondering why she hadn't fed him.

Excusing herself, she hurried into the kitchen and grabbed the bag of dog food from the pantry. She opened the back door and found his bowl, sitting empty on the covered stoop.

"Scooter!" Maryellen called. As she poured Chow-Chow Dog Food into his bowl, she sang his come-to-dinner song: "Chow-Chow Dog Food, Eat it up, And you'll be a happy pup!" That was the Chow-Chow jingle that rang out over television commercials and always brought him running. But when he didn't waddle over, she tried the new jingle she and her mother had made up:

> *Feed Chow-Chow Dog Food to your wolf or pup.*
> *Every breed and size will lap it up.*
> *Then they'll bark for more, more, more.*
> *So hurry and buy some at the store!*

When Scooter still didn't show, Maryellen checked under the bushes and behind the storage shed in the backyard and then hurried to the front yard. The sunny day had turned into a drizzly evening, and she shivered. She looked up and down Palmetto Street, but the street and sidewalks were empty.

Where was Scooter? She thought back to when she had last seen him. It was in the afternoon when she'd tripped over him and shooed him outside.

Had he been gone all that time? Sometimes he visited the neighbors, but he was always home before dinnertime.

Maryellen frowned, worried, and sudden tears pricked her eyes. Scooter never missed a meal, which could mean only one thing—he had run away!

chapter 2
Too Quiet

"SCOOTER'S RUN AWAY!" Maryellen cried out as she ran into the dining room.

No one paid any attention to her. Mrs. Larkin was cutting the cake, and everybody was still talking.

She stomped her foot. "I said *Scooter has run away!*"

"Ellie, dear, you don't have to yell," Mrs. Larkin said as she passed a piece of cake to Mr. Larkin.

Maryellen bit back a sob. "But Scooter's gone!"

Finally everyone looked at her.

"He didn't show up for dinner, and he's not in the yard." Her lower lip began to tremble. "He ran away."

Tom giggled. "Scooter's too fat to run."

"Did you sing him the Chow-Chow song?" Beverly asked. "That worked when he got lost at Yellowstone Park."

16

"Yes, and I rattled the bag, too, and sang our new Chow-Chow song."

"Missing a meal will do him good," Joan said as she forked up a bite of cake. "He's pretty chubby."

"He'll show up." Mrs. Larkin handed Maryellen a plate. "When he didn't get his dinner, he probably wandered down to Miss Nancy's house. She loves to feed him treats."

Mr. Larkin patted Maryellen's shoulder. "Your mother's right. Remember when he hid under Miss Nancy's back porch during that thunderstorm? He didn't come home for hours."

Maryellen swallowed hard. She took the slice of cake and sat down. Everyone else around the table started talking again as if nothing was wrong.

And maybe nothing *was* wrong. Scooter *did* love Miss Nancy, and Maryellen *had* forgotten to feed him. He was probably mad at her and had trotted down to the neighbors'.

But when bedtime came and Scooter still had not

returned home, she began to worry again.

"Your father will call for him before he locks up," Mrs. Larkin said when she tucked Maryellen and Beverly into bed. "I'll phone Miss Nancy, and when your sister gets home I'll have her and Drew walk up and down the street, too. We'll find him, sweetie."

Maryellen snuffled. "Thanks, mom."

When Mrs. Larkin left, Beverly whispered. "Can I come sleep with you? It's too quiet in here without Scooter's snoring."

Maryellen slid to the far side of the mattress. "And lonely, too."

The two snuggled against each other, but it still took Maryellen a long time to fall asleep.

The next morning, Maryellen didn't need her mother to wake her up. She jumped out of bed and raced into the kitchen in her pajamas. "Did Scooter come home?"

Her mother was pouring Wheaties into five bowls and dotting them with sliced banana. She shook her head. "I'm sorry, sweetie, I haven't seen him. Why don't you check and see if he ever ate his dinner?"

Maryellen opened the back door. Scooter's bowl still had the kibble in it she'd poured last night. "His bowl is still full of food. Did Carolyn look for him when she got home?"

Mrs. Larkin nodded. "She and Drew went up and down Palmetto Street, calling until one of the neighbors hollered for them to be quiet."

Mr. Larkin bustled into the kitchen carrying his briefcase and wearing a suit. "Bye kiddos." He kissed Mrs. Larkin and squeezed Maryellen's shoulder. "Scooter will be home by dinnertime," he assured her before leaving for his commute into work. "You know how much he likes to visit the neighbors. He's probably eating a hamburger at Mr. Johnson's house right now."

"Your father's right. So wake up your brothers

and sisters and get dressed for school."

By the time she reached her bedroom, Maryellen was so glum that she barely noticed what she put on.

"You have two different ankle socks on, Ellie-jelly," Carolyn pointed out. "And your blouse has a big chocolate stain on it from last night."

"Who cares," Maryellen grumbled. "It's my fault Scooter is gone."

"Why is it your fault?" Beverly asked, yawning.

"Because I kicked him out of the house yesterday after I tripped over him, and I forgot to feed him on time. He was probably mad, and that's why he ran off to eat a hamburger at the Johnsons'."

"Scooter never gets mad, though he does like hamburger," Carolyn said. "Here's a clean blouse to put on."

Tom and Mikey were already eating when the three girls came into the kitchen. "Scootew's gone!" Mikey cried out in a blubbery voice.

Maryellen slumped into her chair and stared

glumly at the brown flakes in her bowl.

"If he's not home by this afternoon, we'll look for him," Mrs. Larkin said, pouring milk into her bowl. "Now eat your cereal before it gets soggy."

"We'll all look for him," Beverly said. "Like the Happy Hollisters."

Tom stopped chewing. "I want to be Pete."

"I'll be Pam," Beverly said.

"Who are the hoppy Hollistews?" Mikey asked.

"They're a family of detectives," Beverly explained. "They solve mysteries. Right, Maryellen?"

Maryellen shrugged her shoulders. Mom had read *The Happy Hollisters* aloud to her when she was younger, and while the stories weren't as exciting as the Nancy Drew mysteries she read now, the Hollister kids did remind Maryellen of her own big family. If pretending to be the Happy Hollisters got her brothers and sister to help, she'd go along. Plus Beverly was right: If Scooter didn't show up, it would take all of them to find him.

The rain had stopped, so Maryellen decided to ride her bike to school. As she pushed her old two-wheeler from the carport, Davy was just coming out of his house next door.

"I heard everyone calling for Scooter last night," Davy said. "Did you find him?"

Maryellen shook her head. "Did you see him?"

"No. Do you think he's lost?"

"I don't know. Sometimes he visits the neighbors, but he's never been gone this long before."

"I'd help you look this afternoon, but I have basketball practice," said Davy.

Maryellen didn't want to mention that the Happy Hollisters would be helping her, in case Davy might think it was babyish.

"Did you pick a science report topic yet?" Davy asked as he swung onto his sleek black bike and headed up the sidewalk.

"Not yet." Maryellen mounted her own bike but could barely keep up, even pumping hard.

Davy circled in the street and rode up beside her. "I've decided to research codes, like the Morse code."

"Since I had so much fun with the science contest, I was thinking maybe I could do something with rockets." Maryellen sighed. "Right now, though, I don't feel much like lifting off. All I can think of is Scooter wandering around, lost and hungry."

Scooter was on Maryellen's mind all through the school day. During mental math, Miss Dimotsis asked her to solve 132 divided by 12. "Scooter!" popped out of her mouth before she could stop it. Then in English class, Mr. Olivier asked her to summarize the plot of *The Wheel on the School*, a book about Dutch children who try to get storks to return to their fishing village.

"It's about a poor dog lost in Holland," Maryellen announced instead, flushing when she realized her mistake.

After class, her good friend Karen King wrinkled her freckled nose and pressed her palm on

Maryellen's forehead. "I'm checking to see if you have a fever. I think you caught some strange disease that makes you say silly things."

Just then her other two best friends, Karen Stohlman and Angela Terlizzi, hurried over. Maryellen told them all about Scooter.

"Oh, that's terrible!" Karen Stohlman said. Karen was dressed in a brand-new outfit—a lavender circle skirt that whooshed as she walked. Maryellen sometimes found it hard not to feel envious, but today she was only thinking about Scooter.

"I would cry buckets if Amerigo ran off," Angela said. Maryellen's newest friend was from Italy. She wore her long black hair in braids and spoke with a slight accent that Maryellen loved to hear.

"If your family doesn't find him this afternoon, you can count on us to help," Karen King said.

Maryellen thanked them, but inside she told herself she wouldn't need their help because when she got home, Scooter would be waiting. Even if he was muddy from last night's rain, she would give him a giant hug, and she would never shoo him from the house again.

chapter 3

Follow That Truck!

"SCOOTER!" MARYELLEN CALLED.

"Scootew!" Mikey echoed.

The two were trudging up one side of Palmetto Street while Mrs. Larkin, Tom, and Beverly walked up the other. Scooter had not come home. They'd double-checked with Miss Nancy and Mr. Johnson, neither of whom had seen the dog, and now everyone was really worried.

Holding Mikey's hand, Maryellen hurried up the sidewalk to a house that looked just like hers except it had pastel blue shutters instead of green. A tiger cat sat on the stoop, licking its paw. "Hi, Stripey," Maryellen said as she rang the doorbell. The Farrs had two kids younger than Mikey, and sometimes Carolyn babysat for them.

Mrs. Farr opened the door, a baby on her hip.

"Have you seen Scooter, our dachshund?" Maryellen asked, showing Mrs. Farr a black-and-white photo of Scooter that her dad had taken on their vacation the past summer. "He's been missing since yesterday."

"He's fat and bwown. Like a hot dog," Mikey added.

Mrs. Farr squinted at the photo and shook her head. "I'm sorry, kids. We'll keep an eye out for him." A howl came from inside, and with a tired smile, she said good-bye.

Maryellen sighed. "That's the eighth neighbor we've talked to, but no one has seen Scooter. He couldn't just vanish."

"Casper the Fwiendly Ghost can vanish," Mikey declared. He loved the television show about the little cartoon ghost.

Shivers ran up Maryellen's arms, and she clutched her brother's hand tightly. She knew there was no such thing as ghost dogs, but Scooter had definitely disappeared. Finally they reached the corner and met up with the others.

"Any luck?" Maryellen asked hopefully.

Mrs. Larkin shook her head.

"I'm getting tired," Beverly whined. She and Tom had worn roller skates, and had zipped up and down the sidewalks until their faces were red.

"One more block, please?" Maryellen said.

"I've never seen Scooter cross the road," Mrs. Larkin replied, but when Maryellen gave her a pleading look, she added, "Okay, one more block, but then I need to get home and fix dinner."

This time, the group stayed closer together, Maryellen, Mikey, and Beverly taking one house while Mrs. Larkin and Tom took another on the same side of the street.

"Do you know who lives here?" Beverly asked as they hurried up a sidewalk to the stoop in front of a pink stucco house.

"No, but there's an old dog toy in the yard. Maybe Scooter came up to play with this family's dog." Maryellen knocked on the door. A man puffing on a pipe opened it; beside him, a boy about Tom's age peered from under a coonskin cap. "Hi, we're looking for our lost dog," Maryellen said, holding out the photo.

The man studied Scooter's photo. "If you find him, see if he's with our missing Dalmatian. We moved to the neighborhood a month ago, and Spots disappeared two weeks later."

"Do you think he ran off?" Maryellen asked.

The man shook his head. "He's never run off before. We thought he might have gotten lost because he was new to this area. We called the police, but they hadn't received any reports about a stray Dalmatian."

"He's white with black spots all over," the boy said. "That's why we named him Spots."

"Hey, I have spots, too," said Mikey, whose chicken pox spots were still healing.

"Our dog's name is Scooter," called Beverly, who was gliding back and forth behind them on her skates. "He's a dachshund."

Maryellen introduced herself. The man said his name was Mr. Bates, and the boy with the coonskin cap was his son, Louis. Mr. Bates and Maryellen exchanged phone numbers and promised to keep in touch.

Four more houses later, Maryellen was ready to give up. Beverly's crown was lopsided, and Mikey wouldn't stop scratching. When they met up with their mom, Maryellen told them about the Bateses' missing Dalmatian.

"I think we should call the police, too," Maryellen added.

"Good idea," Mrs. Larkin agreed. "Now we really do need to get home."

"Last one to the corner is a rotten egg," Beverly called as she skated off, with Tom in hot pursuit.

Maryellen started to run after them. "No fair! You

two have wheels!" She was running past a telephone
pole when a paper flapping in the wind caught her
attention. On the pole was a poster with a crayon
drawing of a tan dog with floppy ears. The print
under the drawing had faded in the sun and rain, but
Maryellen could still make out what it said: "Have
You Seen Misty?"

"Mom!" Maryellen waved at her mother to hurry.
"Look, there's a *third* missing dog! Right here in our
neighborhood."

Mrs. Larkin frowned. "It does seem odd that
three dogs would run away."

"I wonder if something happened to them?"
Maryellen's eyes widened.

"Like what?" asked Mrs. Larkin.

Maryellen couldn't think of any answer. She'd
heard of bank robbers, but never dog robbers. "I
can't read the phone number. I wonder if Misty is
still missing." Maryellen felt tears well in her eyes. It
was obvious that the poster had been on the pole for

a while. Had the family ever found Misty? And the Bateses' dog had been gone for two weeks. What if Scooter was gone that long? What if they *never* found him?

It was too sad to imagine.

Mikey wrapped his arms around her waist. "Don't cwy, Mawyellen."

Just then the ice cream truck drove around the corner, bell ringing, and parked along the curb. Mr. Brad the ice cream man jumped out, tipped his cap to the Larkins, and opened up the side window. "Who would like a tasty treat?" he called.

"Me. Me!" Mikey pulled away from Maryellen, and Beverly and Tom came speed-skating back.

Maryellen's mouth watered. She was as tired and thirsty as the others, and an ice cream bar sounded heavenly. Mom had a "no treats before dinner" rule, but she said, "You four have worked hard looking for Scooter, so just this one time . . ."

As the truck's bell rang, more children ran up.

Maryellen showed everyone Scooter's photograph, but no one had seen him. Her mom gave her a nickel, and she told Mr. Brad her order: "A fudge bar, please." As she handed him the coin, she remembered that the vendor must know Scooter because he and his truck had parked in the Larkins' driveway and sold treats for Maryellen's birthday.

"Mr. Brad, you drive around the neighborhood. Have you seen our dog?"

He looked at the photo she held out. "Sure. Sometimes I see him when I park near your house." Mr. Brad reached into the truck to find her ice cream bar, and Maryellen stifled a gasp. There were reddish-brown dog hairs *just like Scooter's* on his white uniform.

"Mr. Brad, do you have a dog?" she asked quickly.

"I do. A Westie. That's a West Highland Terrier." He handed her the bar. "But I love all dogs."

"What does your Westie look like?"

"He's little, with wiry white fur."

"You have brown hairs on your sleeve," Maryellen pointed out. "Do you have another dog?"

Mr. Brad's cheeks flushed red as he brushed the hairs off his sleeve. "Um. Uh. Well, like I said, I love all dogs."

Enough to steal one? As she unwrapped her ice cream, Maryellen realized that what she was thinking seemed too silly to say out loud. Or was it? Mr. Brad traveled around The Palms development, so he probably knew every dog. He admitted he knew Scooter, the best dog in the world, and if he wanted to take the dachshund or another dog, he could easily sneak it into his truck. His Westie had white hair, which didn't explain the many reddish-brown hairs on his uniform.

Could there be a dog stashed in the ice cream truck right now? Could *Scooter* be hidden there?

Maryellen's pulse began to race. Taking a bite from the corner of her ice cream bar, she sidled to the front of the truck. There was no door, just a metal step leading straight up to the cab. Keeping one eye on Mr. Brad, who was busy handing out ice cream, she peeked inside. There was no place a dog could be hidden in the small cab, but there was a box of Chow-Chow treats on the floor.

To lure dogs into his truck? Is that what happened to Spots, Misty, and Scooter? Or were they simply treats for his own dog? Frustrated, Maryellen bit hard into her chocolate bar, immediately getting a cold headache. Gosh, she couldn't just blurt out, *Are you stealing dogs from the neighborhood? Did you take Scooter?*

She needed to do a lot more sleuthing to find some answers.

"Mom, can Beverly and I ride bikes before dinner?" Maryellen asked her mother when they started home. "We want to look one more time for Scooter. I promise I'll do the dishes afterward."

"Sure," Mrs. Larkin said, sounding distracted. Mikey had dripped raspberry sherbet on his shirt, his pants—well, just about everywhere—and she was dabbing it with a napkin. "Just stay close by."

"Thanks. Come on, Beverly." Maryellen started jogging toward their house. "The Happy Hollisters have a job to do." Beverly, who was skating next to her, looked puzzled. But since her sister was always happy to tag along, Maryellen knew she'd be up for detective work.

When they reached the carport, Maryellen threw away her ice cream stick and wiped her sticky hands on her pants leg. Beverly sat on the concrete floor and took off her skates. "What are we going to do?" she asked.

"We're going to follow the ice cream truck." Maryellen told her sister about the brown hairs and the dog treats.

"Do you really think that Mr. Brad the ice cream man stole Scooter?" Beverly asked.

Maryellen wrinkled her nose. It did sound sort of crazy. "I don't know what to think. Maybe he just decided he wanted a second dog and Scooter was wandering around outside. It's up to us to follow the clues, and right now those clues point to Mr. Brad." Maryellen pushed her bike from the carport.

"Then let's go." Beverly mounted her own hand-me-down bike, which had training wheels and was even older and slower than Maryellen's. Sleek bikes like Davy's or a Schwinn Starlet sure would have made sleuthing easier. At least the ice cream truck wouldn't be hard to follow. All they had to do was listen for the bell and watch for a swarm of kids.

They found the truck parked on the next block. Maryellen stopped her bike a short distance away and watched as Mr. Brad handed out treats to a dozen kids.

Finally, the kids wandered off, eating their sherbets and cones. As Mr. Brad closed the side window, a brownish-red dog Maryellen didn't recognize trotted over, wagging its tail. "Hey, Buster!" Maryellen could hear him greet the dog. "Are you ready for your treat?" Buster jumped up on Mr. Brad's leg, and the ice cream man gave the dog a friendly pat.

Maryellen's eyes widened as Mr. Brad stepped back and Buster hopped into the open passenger side of the truck.

"Did you see that, Beverly?" she exclaimed. "Now we have proof that Mr. Brad is stealing dogs—which means he must have Scooter!"

chapter 4

Vanishing Tracks

MARYELLEN GRITTED HER teeth in anger. Should she confront the dog thief? Or wait and tell her parents?

Before she could make a decision, Tom came skating down the sidewalk hollering, "Mom says to come home!"

Maryellen whipped her head around and motioned frantically for him to shush so that Mr. Brad wouldn't notice they had followed him. By the time she looked back, the ice cream truck was pulling away.

With Buster in the truck? Maryellen scanned the yards and sidewalks but saw no sign of the big reddish-brown dog. Jumping on her bike, she pedaled after the ice cream truck, but it had already turned the corner and disappeared.

"Mom says *now*," Tom hollered after her.

With a deep sigh, Maryellen braked and rode her bike back up the sidewalk. Tom was already skating back toward home, but Beverly remained almost where Maryellen had left her, hunched over her bike. "You saw that, Beverly, right?" Maryellen asked her sister.

"Saw what?" Beverly straightened.

"Saw that big brown dog hop into Mr. Brad's truck."

"Umm. . ." Beverly's cheeks reddened. "I didn't. My pants leg got caught in my bike chain and I was trying to get it loose without tearing it."

"Phooey!" Maryellen hit the handlebars. "I saw that dog Buster jump into his truck, but I didn't see if he jumped out again because Tom came hollering down the sidewalk." She glanced at the nearby lawns and porches to see if she could spot the dog, but Buster still wasn't in sight. "What if Mr. Brad took him?"

"Why would he? More likely Buster ran home,"

Beverly said, turning her bike. "Which is where we need to be going. Maybe the Happy Hollisters can look for Mr. Brad again tomorrow after school. The ice cream truck usually comes around about then."

"Maybe." Maryellen blew out a frustrated breath. Maybe it was time to call the police and report what she had seen. Only what *had* she seen? Beverly could be right: Buster might have simply run home.

When she got back to her house, Maryellen called Angela and the Karens to let them know Scooter was still missing.

"I'll help you look tomorrow," Karen King said when Maryellen phoned her.

"You must be *soooo* sad," Angela said when Maryellen told her the news.

And Karen Stohlman insisted that calling the police was the right thing to do.

Mr. Larkin helped Maryellen write down important details to tell the Daytona Beach Police Department. Her stomach did flip-flops as she dialed, but her dad gave her an encouraging smile.

She was put through to an Officer Polansky, who took her information. "Other folks have reported pets missing in the area," he told her, "so we've asked the officers to keep an eye out for strays."

"Scooter is not a stray," Maryellen declared. "He has a red collar and a family who loves him." She described the dachshund in detail so that if a policeman did find him, he would know to call the Larkins right away. She thought a moment before adding, "You might want to check with ice cream truck drivers in the area." She knew she couldn't accuse Mr. Brad of anything yet, but she could at least alert the police. "They drive through neighborhoods and may have seen something suspicious."

When she hung up, her father smiled. "Don't look so sad, honey. You did a good job, and I bet by tomorrow, Scooter will be waiting at the back door."

Only he wasn't.

In the morning, the moment Maryellen's eyes

opened, she hurried to the back stoop to check for Scooter. By now the kibble in his bowl was soggy, so she threw it out and washed the bowl.

When Maryellen arrived at school, her friends met her with serious faces.

"We all agreed that if Scooter wasn't home today, we would help you look for him after school," Karen King said.

"I forgot I can't today because I have a piano lesson," Angela said, looking especially glum.

"My mom said she'd pick us up after school and take us to your house," Karen Stohlman said.

Karen King grinned excitedly. "I can't wait to do some detective work just like Nancy Drew!" Now here was a detective worth imitating, Maryellen thought. She and her friends loved Nancy Drew mysteries.

"If only Nancy Drew was real," Karen Stohlman said. "She, George, and Bess would solve 'The Case of the Missing Dachshund' in nothing flat."

The bell rang, and all four girls hurried to their classes with the other students. Maryellen usually loved school, but she couldn't wait for the day to be over so she and her friends could search for Scooter.

That afternoon, the two Karens and Maryellen quickly ate an after-school snack of Wheaties. Maryellen planned on getting her friends to tromp up and down the streets that her family hadn't searched, and she wanted to check on Mr. Brad again, too. The ice cream man was still the perfect suspect— he was always in the neighborhood, he'd admitted he loved dogs, and she'd seen Buster jump into his truck for a treat. She couldn't picture Scooter jumping up into the cab—his legs were too short—but maybe Mr. Brad had helped him inside, getting hairs on his uniform. It made sense, because who wouldn't love a pudgy sweetie pie like Scooter?

"I sure would like to be Nancy Drew," Karen Stohlman said with a sigh.

"No, Maryellen gets to be Nancy. It's her dog,"

Karen King declared.

"I'll be George then," Karen Stohlman said.

"Why do you get to be George? You're not sporty at all," the other Karen argued. "You're more fashionable, like Bess."

"Both of you are Karen, so both of you can be Nancy or George or whoever you want," Maryellen said. She wanted them to hurry and change so they could get outside. Mrs. Larkin had taken the younger kids with her to the supermarket, so for once they weren't hanging around. But there was only an hour and a half before Mrs. Stohlman would be back to pick her friends up.

Karen King put her hands on her hips. "I vote we all be Nancy then."

"I second the motion," Karen Stohlman said. "Now we'll need to look for clues. Do you have a magnifying glass?" she asked Maryellen.

"Somewhere in that old science kit." Maryellen pointed to a torn box in her closet, and Karen

Stohlman started to rummage in it.

"And we need disguises!" Karen King exclaimed.

Maryellen frowned. "Disguises?"

"Of course! If Mr. Brad the ice cream guy sees you snooping around again, don't you think he'll get suspicious?"

Maryellen thought a minute. "Not if we're buying ice cream. . . . I have twenty cents saved from my allowance."

But Karen King was already using Carolyn's lipstick and mascara. "With a little makeup, we'll look like teenagers, not twerpy fifth-graders."

"Carolyn's not going to like you using her stuff," Maryellen warned. "And I'm not allowed to wear makeup until I'm fifteen."

"But we're older than fifteen." Karen King grinned, the smudge of red around her lips making her smile look as huge as a clown's. "We're Nancy Drew, remember?"

"Look! I found a magnifying glass. Now we need

a flashlight," Karen Stohlman said, backing out from the closet.

"It's daylight out," Maryellen protested.

"We might get locked in a dark room," Karen Stohlman said in a spooky voice.

"Then we better have a whistle, too," Karen King said, "in case we have to call for help. And a pad of paper to write down all our clues."

"And a camera to take photos of suspicious characters. Hey, I want a disguise, too!" Karen Stohlman said when she saw her friend's made-up face.

Maryellen rubbed her forehead. She loved the Karens, and they had some good ideas, but if they didn't hurry, they'd never get any sleuthing done. "Mom keeps a flashlight in the kitchen in case the power goes out. Tom has a toy whistle. I can't use Dad's camera—he's afraid we kids will break it. I have a school notepad that will fit in my pocket and a pencil. Now, let's hurry before you have to leave."

It took ten minutes of hunting in the boys' room

before Karen King finally found Tom's whistle under his pillow. She tried it out as they clattered downstairs. Maryellen found the flashlight, and finally got her two friends outside.

"What time does the ice cream truck come around?" Karen Stohlman asked.

"I think we should knock on doors," Karen King said. "Maybe a lonely little old lady has Scooter and is feeding him steak so he doesn't want to leave."

Maryellen was torn about what they should do first. "Let's go to Beachside Street. My family didn't check there, and Scooter can cut through our backyard to get to it. If the ice cream truck comes by, we'll check out Mr. Brad again."

"Good plan, Nancys!" the Karens chorused.

"Wait—I'd better leave my mom a note." Maryellen ran inside the house.

By the time she ran back outside, Mrs. Stohlman was waiting on the curb.

The two Karens hurried past her and into the

house to get their school clothes and books. "Sorry, we have to go," Karen King apologized.

Karen Stohlman gave Maryellen an encouraging pat on the shoulder as she left. "You're still Nancy Drew, so keep investigating!"

Maryellen waved good-bye, not quite believing that they'd spent the entire time time getting ready to be detectives. She turned toward the house with a frustrated sigh, and then stopped midstep. Her friends had given her some good ideas. The afternoon hadn't been a total waste.

She tucked the flashlight into her waistband and shoved the whistle in the pocket of her pedal pushers along with the twenty cents she'd put there earlier. Then, sitting on the front step, she began to write in her notebook.

For her first entry, Maryellen put yesterday's date and wrote down what the Happy Hollisters had discovered:

Spots: the Bateses' Dalmatian missing for two weeks
Misty: brown and white dog missing for how long??
Mr. Brad: dog hairs on his uniform
    Chow-Chow treats in truck
    loves dogs
    drives all over the neighborhood
    lured Buster into his truck and may have taken him
Officer Polansky: other dogs reported missing too

When she finished, Maryellen realized that she had quite a lot of information. Only none of it told her exactly where Scooter was.

How would Nancy Drew find a missing pet? Of course—she'd try to find its trail. Yesterday they'd been so busy hunting up and down the neighborhood, they'd never checked for tracks.

Maryellen ran into the house and out onto the back steps. No one had played in the backyard since Scooter had gone missing. Using the flashlight and magnifying glass, she searched for paw prints. She

remembered it had drizzled the night he disappeared, which could have washed away tracks, so she
would have to search carefully.

She found ants crawling up the steps to some
spilled kibble, and an earthworm squirming in the
moist earth. But there were no Scooter tracks around
the steps or leading into the backyard. That meant he
probably hadn't gone toward Beachside Street.

She wrote her findings on her pad and then hurried to the front porch. When she'd let Scooter out the
front door, it was the last time she'd seen him.

Carefully, she looked around the steps and down
the Larkins' walkway. There would be no prints *in*
the concrete, she knew, but maybe there was a muddy
one *on* it that the light rain hadn't washed away.

She made her way down the length of the walkway until it met the main sidewalk. *Nothing.* It was as
if Scooter had disappeared into thin air.

Or turned into a ghost like Casper.

Maryellen plopped dejectedly on the curb. If

Scooter were here, he'd be playing her faithful sleuthing partner who could track lost kittens and, well, lost *dogs*. He would have helped her solve his own disappearance in a finger snap.

She sighed, missing him with an ache. *Don't give up,* she told herself as she got to her feet. *Scooter depends on you.*

Taking baby steps, she made her way down the sidewalk along the street, searching for a sign of where he might have gone. Suddenly, she gasped. *Muddy paw prints!*

They came from the direction of the Larkins' grassy front yard, crossed the sidewalk, and then disappeared right at the curb. Maryellen checked the prints carefully with her magnifying glass. They were faded and slightly dried, and about the size of Scooter's paws. Had he crossed the street to the other side? Her stomach did a flip-flop. She really hoped he hadn't. The speed limit was only twenty miles an hour, but the street was still no place for a little dog.

She used the flashlight to search the asphalt and found no sign of prints in the road. She blew out a relieved breath but then frowned in confusion. It was as if Scooter had stopped at the curb and then . . . flown into the sky?

Or been lifted from the curb and put into an ice cream truck!

Maryellen clenched her fists. Mr. Brad said he often parked in front of the Larkins' house. She knew what she needed to do next.

It was time to confront the ice cream man.

chapter 5

Something Odd

TOO MANY CLUES pointed to Mr. Brad. Sitting on the curb, Maryellen jotted down her findings. As she slipped the notepad into her pocket, her mother pulled into the driveway.

Mikey was crying, and Tom was arguing with Beverly as the two got out of the station wagon. "You took my lollipop," he accused her.

"Did not!"

"Did too!"

Mrs. Larkin climbed out the driver's side, looking tired. Maryellen knew it was the wrong time to run off and be a detective. Instead, she helped her mom carry in the bags of groceries.

"Will you run an oatmeal bath for Mikey?" Mrs. Larkin asked. "He can't stop scratching. Your father is working late, so it's an early supper of tomato soup and grilled cheese for you kids."

"Yum, my favorites." Maryellen took her little brother's hand. "Come on, Tonto. We'll pretend the Lone Ranger and his trusted sidekick have to dive in a lake and swim across to rescue . . ."

"Scootew!" Mikey chimed in. "He doesn't like the watew."

Maryellen raised one brow. Scooter couldn't have gone all the way to the beach, could he? He often went with the family in the summer and fall when the water was still warm enough to swim, but he had never waddled that far on his own, and the trail of prints had stopped practically in front of their house. Still, anything could have happened, she realized. Maybe she had jumped to conclusions about Mr. Brad and wasn't looking at other possibilities. She hoped that after dinner she would have a chance to find out one way or another about the ice cream truck driver.

Maryellen was washing the last of the soup bowls

when the ice cream truck bell jangled from outside. "That's Mr. Brad, just in time for dessert. Is it all right if I treat the others?" she asked her mother, remembering the twenty cents she had in her pocket.

"Thanks, sweetie. Keep them outside while they eat their ice cream. That will give me time to put away the last of the groceries."

Whooping, the four kids ran out to the ice cream truck, which Mr. Brad had pulled up to the curb in front of the Larkins' house. Maryellen noticed that the muddy prints that went across the sidewalk led right to the spot where he'd parked.

"Ice cream! Yummy goodies!" Mr. Brad tipped his hat. "Hello, my best customers!"

Maryellen barely smiled at him before handing Beverly, Mikey, and Tom each a nickel. "Keep him busy," she whispered to Beverly.

In a dramatic voice, Beverly said, "I would like an orange sherbet. No, make that a strawberry slurp. Oh, wait, do you have any chocolate gooey bars?"

While Beverly placed her order, Maryellen snuck around the front of the truck to the driver's side door. She opened it, trying to be quiet, and slipped into the seat. Leaning over to the passenger side, she checked for paw prints on the floor and seat. While she investigated, she listened for the *ching-ching* of Mr. Brad's change dispenser so she knew he was still busy.

The Chow-Chow box was on the seat, and crumbs littered the floor as if a dog had munched on a treat inside. The floorboard and step down were covered with sand and a few wrappers, and she spotted a dog print that looked bigger than Scooter's. Maybe Buster's?

"Phooey," Maryellen muttered, disappointed that she hadn't found any clues that indicated Scooter had been in the truck. It was possible that there were no clues because Mr. Brad had cleaned it since the day the dachshund had disappeared, but Maryellen didn't think it was likely. The interior looked pretty grubby.

She heard Beverly's voice rise shrilly. "Thank you, Mr. Brad, for all your help."

That was her cue to leave. Maryellen sneaked out of the truck as quietly as she had entered and ran around the back bumper to the passenger side, where Mr. Brad was shutting the freezer.

She held out her nickel. "A chocolate crunch, please," she said, and as the ice cream vendor opened the freezer again, she added, "Mr. Brad, you said you often see Scooter when you park here. What about yesterday?"

Mr. Brad rubbed his chin. "Let's see . . . not yesterday. But I did see him the day before. You kids didn't come out, but Scooter was sitting on the front steps. He hopped down to greet me, and I gave him a treat."

"Did he jump in your truck?" Maryellen asked.

Mr. Brad reddened. "In my truck? Um, well . . . no. The company has strict rules about our vehicles. I give the dogs Chow-Chow treats before I leave. That way they're busy chewing and not following me or going into the street. Scooter was on the curb eating his when I drove off."

He is definitely not telling the truth! Maryellen thought. She'd seen Buster jump into his truck with her own eyes. How could she get him to admit it?

"You know, there are three missing dogs in this neighborhood, including Scooter. It's almost as if someone *stole* them," she said, hoping his expression might look guilty.

"That's terrible!" he exclaimed, looking distressed. "I love all the dogs on my route. Do you have any idea what happened to them?"

"No. They just vanished. I was hoping since you drive around the neighborhood that you might have noticed something unusual."

Mr. Brad handed her the crunch bar and took her nickel. Then he tipped his hat back and thought for a second. "Well, there is something odd," he said finally. "Sometimes I see a tan station wagon in the neighborhood with a sign on the side door that says

'Barkhaven.' It was parked in front of your neighbor's house two days ago. When I drove away, it pulled up. Scooter was still at the curb, but I didn't think anything of it."

"Barkhaven?" Maryellen repeated. "I've never heard of it."

"I've never heard of it either," Mr. Brad added. "Now I've got to be off. Good luck finding your pup."

Maryellen had never seen a tan station wagon outside her house, and she already knew that Mr. Brad had lied about Buster. Could he be making up a story to throw her off the track?

She needed to find out, that was for sure.

That night, Maryellen sped through her math problems and the last chapter in *The Wheel on the School*, hoping there would be time before bed to look through the phone book, which might tell her whether there really was a "Barkhaven" or if Mr.

Brad was telling her a fishy tale.

It was almost bedtime when Maryellen opened the Daytona Beach phone directory and turned to the business listings printed on the yellow pages in the back. She flipped through, checking under the headings "Pets" and "Animals." Finally she found a Bark Haven under "Animal Rescue." It was the only one listed. Did the tan station wagon belong to the rescue organization? Had Mr. Brad really seen it? If so, did it pick up Scooter that day? And why would anyone think her dog needed rescuing? Scooter was well fed and wore a red collar.

She wrote all the new information she'd discovered in her notebook. Now there were two pages of clues. Tomorrow she needed to check out this Bark Haven, which might help her decide whether Mr. Brad was telling the truth. Closing the phone book, she decided to ask Davy if he'd go with her. Davy wouldn't spend time arguing about who was going to be Nancy Drew.

Slipping outside, Maryellen made her way to the

Fenstermachers' house and rapped on Davy's half-open window: *Tap, tappety, tap, tap. Tap, tap.*

Davy threw open his window. With a grin, he held up a book he'd been reading titled *Communication Through the Ages.*

"Is that helping you research your science report?" Maryellen asked.

Davy nodded. "Yeah, it's about how soldiers used different ways to talk to each other during World War Two, like radio telegraphy. What's up?"

"Plenty. Scooter still hasn't come home. It's been two days. I've been doing lots of detective work, but I need a partner." She recited the clues she'd written in her notebook, ending with Bark Haven. "I need to check out the place. Will you come with me?"

Davy didn't hesitate. "Yes! Tomorrow after school we'll ride our bikes to Bark Haven. I bet they picked up Scooter by mistake."

Maryellen's spirits rose. "Do you think so?"

"Well, let's hope so," Davy replied with conviction.

Just then Mrs. Fenstermacher's voice rang from the doorway. "Davy?"

"Oops. Gotta go. See you later, alligator."

Before she could say "after a while, crocodile," he'd shut the window. Maryellen hurried back home and slid into bed moments before Mrs. Larkin came in with Beverly to tuck the two girls in for the night.

Maryellen told her mother about Bark Haven and asked her to call the organization in the morning to ask about Scooter, since she'd be in school.

"Of course I will," said Mom. "Oh, I bet that's where Scooter is, waiting for us to pick him up." She pulled the covers up to Maryellen's chin. "You've done some excellent detective work. It can't be long before we find Scooter and bring him home. And when we do, we'll tackle the Jell-O jingle contest. The winner gets a trip to New York City."

"Wow—New York!" Maryellen had dreamed of Times Square with its bright lights and Broadway musicals. "'Hello, wiggly, jiggly Jell-O. You sure are swell-o. With your colors of red, green, and yellow!'"

Mrs. Larkin laughed. "You've still got the knack, Ellie. Or maybe I should call you Ell-o!"

Maryellen laughed, then asked, "When do you think we'll hear from the Schwinn contest? I'm tired of pedaling that old bike."

"This week, I hope. Meanwhile, I'm keeping my fingers crossed about Scooter and Bark Haven." Mrs. Larkin clicked off the light as she left.

Maryellen snuggled deeper into her pillow and smiled. Not because of the silly rhyme or winning a prize, but because with Davy's help she just knew she'd find Scooter tomorrow.

When Maryellen got home from school the next day, Mrs. Larkin reported that even though she'd called Bark Haven three times, no one had answered.

"Davy and I are riding out there," Maryellen said. "According to the phone book, it's on Sandy Lane, which isn't too far."

"Tom has a dentist appointment or I would drive you." Mrs. Larkin helped her find the street on a map and made her promise that she and Davy would stick together and be home before dinner.

When Maryellen came around the corner of the house and saw that Davy was riding his bike in the street with Wayne, she stifled a groan. Wayne and Davy were good friends, and they were all in fifth grade together, but Wayne's teasing was *so* annoying—and besides, she hadn't invited him along.

As Maryellen pushed her bike down the drive, she heard the two arguing while riding circles around each other. "*I'm* going to be Sergeant Joe Friday," Davy said, "the greatest cop in Los Angeles."

"No, I'm Friday," Wayne said. "You're Officer Frank Smith, his partner."

"Why am I Smith?" Davy asked.

"Because you're younger than me," Wayne replied.

"Just by two months," Davy countered. "And my

bike is faster and I'm a better football player."

"Yeah, but I was better at making baskets at practice yesterday."

"What does that have to do with being a police officer?"

"What does football?"

"Stop it, you two!" Maryellen hollered. She wasn't going to have another afternoon like yesterday's mess with the Karens. "This is not an episode of *Dragnet* on TV. We have to concentrate on finding Scooter." Davy nodded. "I told Wayne all about the case, so he's ready to help."

"Okay, okay," Maryellen grumbled. She had to admit that three detectives probably were better than two. "But no more arguing."

"I agree—right, Officer Smith?" Davy said to Wayne.

"You mean, 'right, Sergeant Friday,'" Wayne shot back, and then he said in a TV voice, "This is my city— Daytona Beach, Florida. I work here. I'm a cop. It was

Thursday, three thirty-four p.m. My partner, Frank Smith, and I . . ."

"You mean my partner, Sergeant Friday," Davy cut in.

"You know what? *I'm* going to be Sergeant Joe Friday," Maryellen said. She took off, hoping to leave them behind, but their bikes were twice as fast as her clunker, and the boys sped past her.

Maryellen gritted her teeth. She couldn't wait to win that Schwinn Starlet. Then she'd be the leader and leave them in her dust—*really* in the dust, since Sandy Lane wasn't paved, and she was soon enveloped in a cloud kicked up by the boys' tires.

"You made it, Sergeant Slowpoke," Wayne said when she finally caught up at Bark Haven. The boys had already dismounted and put down their kickstands.

Maryellen leaned her bike against a palm tree and looked up the lane at a low concrete block building, surrounded by green grass and shaded by trees.

She could see fenced kennels sticking out behind the building and even from this distance she could hear a chorus of barking and howls.

Crossing her fingers that Scooter was one of the dogs making all that noise, she headed toward the front door. She passed an old blue pickup truck with "Bark Haven" painted on its side panel in white letters. Mr. Brad had described a tan station wagon, but maybe the organization had more than one rescue vehicle.

A bell over the door rang when they entered, and a young woman looked up from a cluttered desk. "Welcome to Bark Haven, Daytona Beach's only dog rescue organization. I'm Miss Hopkins. How can I help you?"

"Hi. We're looking for my dog, Scooter, who went missing on Monday," said Maryellen. She described the dachshund and showed Miss Hopkins the black-and-white photo. "He was wearing a red collar."

"And he is definitely too chubby to be mistaken

for a stray," Davy chimed in.

"Sometimes we do pick up lost dogs. Let me check my records." Miss Hopkins opened a ledger and ran her finger down the entries. "He disappeared three days ago?"

Maryellen nodded.

"According to my records," Miss Hopkins said, "we have not picked up any dogs in your area in the past week."

"What about any dachshunds?" Maryellen asked. Maybe Scooter had wandered out of the neighborhood and been picked up somewhere else.

"Nope. Let me get your name and phone number in case he shows up." Miss Hopkins shut the ledger and picked up a pen.

Maryellen's hopes plummeted. She'd been certain they would find Scooter here, because if he wasn't here, where in the world was he? Sighing, she gave Miss Hopkins her name, address, and phone number.

Wayne pointed toward the door in the back of the

room. "Can we check the kennels?"

Miss Hopkins shot them a suspicious look. "Absolutely not. Visitors are not allowed in the kennels. Now I checked our records and told you there are no dachshunds here," she said firmly. "I'll let you know if we find Scooter." She practically pushed the three kids out the front door.

Once outside, Davy said, "Boy, she sure wanted to get rid of us."

"Especially when you asked to see the kennels, Wayne," Maryellen said. "I wonder if she's hiding something—like a dog named Scooter."

"If Scooter was here, why would she lie about it?" Davy asked.

"I don't know," Maryellen admitted. "But let's face it, this whole thing is a mystery. Did Scooter run away? Is he lost? Did someone take him?" She glanced at the closed door of Bark Haven, then looked back at Davy and Wayne. "Now, I want you two to do some real detective work," she whispered.

"Distract Miss Hopkins so I can sneak around in back and check for myself that Scooter is not here."

"Aye, aye, Sergeant Slowpoke!" Wayne said. He and Davy saluted Maryellen and hurried back inside the building. She could hear them asking Miss Hopkins where else to check for missing dogs. Crouching low when she passed the only window, Maryellen ran around back. Five long, fenced-in runs stretched from the rear of the building. Each run had an opening that led into the building, and each held dogs.

When the dogs saw her, they jumped on the fences or twirled in circles, barking frantically. Maryellen looked nervously toward the front of the building, worried that the added noise would attract Miss Hopkins's attention. Maryellen hurried along the fence, crossing her fingers that the boys could keep Miss Hopkins occupied long enough for Maryllen to finish looking for Scooter.

In the pens behind the building were mutts of all

sizes, a German shepherd, two cocker spaniels, two terriers, and three hounds. She saw no Dalmatian or dachshund, and nothing like floppy-eared Misty.

Maryellen stuck her fingers between the chain links and told the dogs that they were all good puppies. They whined and licked and wiggled. The kennels were clean and the pens had bowls of water, toys, and shade, but still Maryellen's heart ached. It was so sad that these dogs didn't have homes. At least Scooter had a home and a family who loved him.

When she reached the last kennel and hadn't found the missing dachshund, Maryellen's shoulders slumped. Bark Haven was one more clue leading nowhere.

She bit back a sob. *Oh, Scooter, where are you?*

chapter 6

High Hopes

"EXCUSE ME, YOUNG lady!"

Maryellen whirled to see Miss Hopkins storming around the corner of the building, Davy and Wayne trotting behind with apologetic expressions on their faces. "You don't have permission to be back here."

Maryellen stepped away from the fence. "I'm sorry. I was just looking for Scooter."

Miss Hopkins set her fists on her hips. "I told you he wasn't here. Now you are needlessly riling up the dogs." She cast a nervous glance over her shoulder, as if someone might be watching. "You need to leave, right now."

"Right. Okay." With her head ducked, Maryellen hurried past Miss Hopkins. When she reached the side of the building, she broke into a run, with Davy and Wayne following right behind her.

Without a word, the three jumped on their bikes and raced down Sandy Lane until they reached the paved road.

"Whew!" Davy stopped first. "Miss Hopkins was sure mad when she saw you."

"Why didn't you keep her busy?" Maryellen asked, braking beside him.

"We did until she got annoyed with all our questions, and told us to leave, too. Then she heard the dogs going crazy. She muttered something about having enough enemies already, and ran outside. Did you find Scooter?"

Maryellen shook her head sadly. "I was so hoping he'd be there. Did Miss Hopkins know anything about Misty or Spots?"

"No, but she sure acted nervous," Wayne said. "She avoided our questions as if she was hiding something. And get this: Bark Haven does *not* have a station wagon according to Miss Hopkins. She seemed puzzled when we asked her about it."

"Gee, that *is* interesting," said Maryellen. "She might be lying—or Mr. Brad might be the one telling us a big fish tale."

The three mounted their bikes again and rode only a short distance before Wayne stopped again, gesturing wildly. "The ice cream truck just zipped around the corner and headed into our neighborhood!"

"This is our chance to catch him in the act of stealing a dog!" Maryellen said. "I definitely saw Buster get into his truck, although I don't know for sure that Mr. Brad actually took him."

"I think we should look for the mysterious station wagon," Davy said. "If you ask me, that's more suspicious than a guy who drives an ice cream truck."

"Only no one has seen the station wagon except Mr. Brad," Maryellen protested.

"My point exactly," Davy argued. "If we find the Barkhaven station wagon, we know Mr. Brad was telling the truth and Miss Hopkins is not."

Wayne shook his head. "If we nab Mr. Brad in the act, we'll know he's *not* telling the truth. And that's what I'm going to do." Jumping on his bike, Wayne sped off.

"Let him go," Davy said when Maryellen started after him. "Maybe it's best that we split up. We can cover more ground that way."

"But if Wayne finds something important, we won't know," Maryellen said with a frown. "I wish there was a way to talk with each other. Like a can on both ends of a string that goes from bike to bike."

"Or radio telegraphy."

Maryellen gave Davy a puzzled look.

He smiled. "That's what I was researching for my science report, remember?" he said. "It's a way to communicate over long distances using radio waves and Morse code. Dot-dash-dot kind of thing."

"Well, we don't have radio whatever," Maryellen said. "But let's try to find that station wagon."

"I'm with you." Davy got on his bike. "If Mr. Brad is telling the truth, there may be criminals cruising the area looking for dogs and bringing them to Bark Haven."

"But why would anyone take a dog that obviously belongs to someone?" Maryellen asked as she put one foot on her pedal. "And why would Bark Haven want stolen dogs? Most people buy puppies from pet shops, and we got Scooter from a breeder."

Davy shrugged. "I don't know, but right now, nothing makes sense."

"That's for sure," Maryellen agreed as the two set off down the road and glided back into The Palms, Maryellen's neighborhood of pastel-colored houses and lawns dotted with palm trees. They rode down street after street, looking for a tan station wagon. The sun was getting lower, and Maryellen was starting to worry that they wouldn't find the station wagon before they had to go home for dinner, when a tan vehicle cruised right past them with the word "Barkhaven" written on its side. She caught her breath. "There it is!" she exclaimed. "Mr. Brad was right!"

They hurried to catch up as the station wagon paused at a stop sign. They stayed far enough behind the station wagon so the driver wouldn't get suspicious.

When the car abruptly pulled over to the curb in front of a light green house with yellow shutters, Davy and Maryellen stopped, too. Maryellen laid her bike on the grass next to a parked car so the man in the station wagon couldn't see it. "I'm going to try to get closer and find out what they're up to," she whispered to Davy. "Be ready to chase after them if they drive off."

Peering around the car, she could see that the station wagon's passenger-side door was open, and a man wearing a flannel shirt was leaning out. He had a scraggly beard and a ball cap pulled low on his forehead, and he held something in his outstretched hand.

Maryellen craned her neck—a collie was lying in the front yard of the green house where the station wagon had stopped. The dog was eyeing the man's hand, so she figured he must be holding a treat. Then she heard the man whistle and call, "Here, boy."

The dog stood up, wagging its tail. Maryellen blinked. Was the man trying to lure the collie over to him?

Then the sound of whining drew her gaze to the back of the station wagon, where a different dog was pressing its nose against the back window. Maryellen couldn't tell what breed it was, but it was staring at her with frightened eyes.

"Good boy! Come on over here," the man said, waving the treat. The collie stood up and trotted closer to the station wagon.

Maryellen's palms began to sweat. She had to do something. If these men *were* dog thieves, she couldn't let them steal this family's dog. She popped up from behind the parked car and began walking toward the dog as if she knew him. "Hello, Rex, how are you?" she called, trying to sound casual.

Instantly the station wagon door slammed, and with squealing tires, the car took off. Davy took off, too. Maryellen knew he wouldn't be able to catch up on his bike, but maybe he could get a license plate number.

The collie greeted her with a friendly lick. Maryellen sighed with relief that the bearded man hadn't lured the dog into the station wagon. But what if the men came back? Should she warn the family that their dog was the target of robbers?

Hurrying up the walkway to the house, she knocked on the door. A teenage boy answered. He held a transistor radio to his ear and was snapping his fingers. Maryellen told him what happened.

"Right-o," he said, shutting the door on her and the collie.

He doesn't even care! Maryellen fumed. No wonder dogs were so easily taken. No, that isn't quite fair, she quickly realized. Scooter might have jumped into someone's car too, and her family *did* care.

By the time she got back to her bike, Davy was pedaling down the street toward her. "Lost 'em!" he gasped. His face was red and he was breathing hard. "The car zoomed off when it left The Palms and took off into town. I would have followed it, but the road was too busy. Maybe the police will catch them for speeding."

"So far, the police haven't done anything to find out what's going on with the missing dogs," Maryellen grumbled.

"They might have to do something now." Davy grinned. "I got the license plate number." He tapped his head. "Stored it right up here in the old noggin. We'll call Officer Polansky as soon as we get home."

"Finally, real evidence!" Maryellen grinned back. Davy told her the number, and she wrote it in her notebook. "If the police find the driver of the station wagon, maybe it will lead us to Scooter."

"I noticed something odd about the station wagon," Davy said. "On the sign at the building and on the pickup truck's door, 'Bark Haven' is two words. But the sign on the station wagon is only one word."

"Hmm." Maryellen frowned. "Maybe it's not the same rescue organization as the one we visited."

"Or maybe the thieves can't spell."

"Either way, I'll make sure to give that information to Officer Polansky, too," Maryellen said.

Just then, Wayne's booming voice rang down the street. "Officer Smith! Sergeant Slowpoke!"

Maryellen couldn't help rolling her eyes.

"Did you find out anything?" Davy asked Wayne when he braked in front of them.

"I found where Mr. Brad lives. I followed his truck to an apartment house on Tenth Street, which is near our neighborhood. And I heard a dog barking inside!"

"Did it sound like Scooter?" Maryellen was so excited she forgot all about the station wagon.

"Well, it was a dog," said Wayne. "I think we need to do some surveillance."

"Maybe, but it turns out Mr. Brad was telling the truth about the station wagon," Davy said. They told Wayne all about the man trying to lure the collie into the Barkhaven station wagon, and about the funny way its sign was spelled.

"That sounds mighty suspicious," Wayne said. "Still, what if that dog I heard is Scooter?"

Maryellen hated to agree with Wayne, but he had a point. "Okay, let's check it out." Tucking the notebook in her pocket, she swung onto her bike.

Wayne led the way from The Palms onto a side street. He stopped in front of a three-story apartment house painted pink, with striped awning over the front door. The ice cream truck was parked between two cars in a small lot next to the apartment house.

"What now?" Davy asked as they stared at the building.

Maryellen wasn't sure herself. She held her breath,

listening, but she didn't hear any barking.

"Let's go inside and knock on all the doors," Wayne said, getting off his bike.

"Dumb idea," Davy called, but Wayne was already sprinting to the front door. Maryellen watched as he pulled on the knob; she could see that it was locked.

Wayne sauntered back. "Okay, dumb idea."

Maryellen noticed mailboxes tucked in the alcove. "Let's find out which apartment is Mr. Brad's and then ring the bell to his apartment. If Scooter is in there, he'll bark."

"Now that's a good idea," Davy said.

"No, it's a dumb idea," Wayne said. "Even if we hear Scooter, we can't barge in to get him. If Mr. Brad did steal him, he's not going to admit it or let us inside."

"Mr. Brad has to come outside sometime," Maryellen said, propping her bike against a tree in front of the building. "I'll wait for him—even if it takes forever. Well, at least I'll wait until dinnertime, when Mom expects me home—then I'll confront him and demand to see Scooter."

"Not by yourself, you won't," Davy said as the three went to the front door.

Maryellen scanned the mail slots. Each one had a round doorbell, an apartment number, and a last name. "Oh no—I don't know Mr. Brad's last name. It's not on his uniform name tag."

"Then let's ring all the bells!" Wayne elbowed her aside and began punching each button.

"Wayne, stop! We're going to get in big trouble," Davy said.

"You want to find her dog, don't you?" Wayne retorted.

A sound from above caught Maryellen's attention. She stepped out from under the awning to see a window on the second floor fly open and a woman with curlers in her hair lean out. "What do you want?" the woman yelled.

"Mr. Brad, the ice cream man!" Maryellen called back, but the lady ducked away from the window with no reply.

Suddenly, Maryellen heard the faint sound of frantic barking coming from the open window.

chapter 7
A Close Call

"LISTEN, YOU GUYS!" Maryellen cried. "Can you hear the barking?"

Wayne stopped punching doorbells for a second. Davy hurried from the alcove to stand beside Maryellen.

Yip, yap, yap, yip, she heard from the open window, though it was faint, as if coming from the second floor. The bark was too shrill for a big dog like Buster, but Mr. Brad had said he had a Westie, so Maryellen realized it could be from a small terrier. Still, it sounded enough like Scooter that she cupped her hands around her mouth and called up toward the open window, "Scooter! It's me!" She hoped that if it was the dachshund he would bark louder in return.

A window went up on the third floor. "You kids

better scram before I call the police," an older woman with gray hair called down.

"Please, ma'am," Maryellen called back, "we just want to know if Mr. Brad the ice cream man has a brown dachshund in his apartment."

"No, he has a little white thing, I think," the woman replied.

"Does he have only one dog?" Maryellen persisted.

Suddenly the front door opened, and a man with tattoos on his forearms and a fierce scowl came out onto the stoop. Wayne and Davy scurried down the steps to the sidewalk, stumbling in their hurry to get away from him.

"Why are you brats hollering and ringing door-bells?" he growled. "This is a peaceful place, and I sleep days and you woke me up."

Maryellen's heart leapt into her throat, but she wasn't going to let the man's angry expression scare her off. "I—I'm looking for my dog," she stammered as the three backed away from him. "He's a brown dachshund."

"Whadda you think this is—a dog pound?" the man asked curtly. "Go bother people someplace else."

"But sir, my dog—"

"Beat it! No dachshunds here."

"Come on, Maryellen." Davy tugged on her arm when the man waved a threatening fist. "He's not going to help us."

Whirling, Maryellen raced down the sidewalk after Davy and Wayne. She tripped over a potted plant, running into Davy, who slammed into Wayne. The three fell in a heap of arms and legs. Fortunately, the tattooed man didn't come after them but only stood on the steps, glaring.

"Sorry for bothering you, sir!" Maryellen yelled over her shoulder as she scrambled to her feet. Her heart pounding furiously, she mounted her bike and pedaled after Wayne and Davy, who were already halfway down Tenth Street. She finally caught up with them in front of Big Dot's Soda Shop.

"Wow, that was a doozy of a close call!" Wayne exclaimed as he jumped off his bike.

Maryellen wiped the sweat off her forehead. Her ankle throbbed where she'd hit it on the plant pot. It may have been a close call, but for what? They still didn't know anything more than they had before. "Why are we stopping here? We need to go back to that apartment and find out for sure if Mr. Brad has Scooter."

"I'm not going back there until that goon leaves for work or goes to sleep or something," Wayne said. "Besides, he told us there was no dachshund there."

"He probably said that to get rid of us," Davy said.

"Well, I'm too pooped to pop." Wayne pulled a dollar bill from his pocket. "How about if we try again after a soda? My treat."

Maryellen's mouth began to water at the thought of a root beer float. Maybe chasing the dog thieves could wait for a little while.

"When we do, no more ringing bells and hollering," Davy suggested. "There's got to be some way to find out Mr. Brad's last name or apartment number."

"We may just have to stake out the place until dinnertime," Maryellen said.

"Then we'll definitely need refreshment," said Wayne.

Inside Big Dot's, Maryellen limped into the ladies' room and washed her hands. She stared at her image in the mirror. Dust streaked her cheeks, and her hair stuck up every which way. She'd scraped her shin stumbling over the pot, and her knees ached from pedaling so hard. All that effort, and she still hadn't found Scooter.

So much for being an ace investigator. She doubted that Nancy Drew ever looked so untidy or took so long to solve such an important case.

She joined Davy and Wayne on the stools at the counter and gave Big Dot her order. "Root beer float with vanilla ice cream." Davy ordered a chocolate malt, and Wayne asked for a banana split.

Maryellen took a giant sip of her float when it came. The fizzy, creamy drink was just what she needed. "Yum. This was a good idea, Wayne. I'm tired, too, from biking after dognappers."

"The big question is—why do thieves want to steal dogs?" Davy asked. "It's not like stealing money from a bank."

Maryellen frowned. "I asked that same question earlier. If we find the answer, maybe we'll also find Scooter and the other missing dogs."

"I say we head back to Bark Haven and confront Miss Hopkins with what we discovered," Davy said. "Maybe she has an explanation for the Barkhaven name on the station wagon."

"Miss Hopkins did act suspicious," Maryellen said. "Could be she's the leader of the dog stealing gang."

"Or Mr. Brad is," Wayne said as he spooned a giant chunk of banana and ice cream into his mouth.

"I say we stake out his apartment," he mumbled, his mouth full.

"Wayne might be right," Davy said. "Mr. Brad could be the lookout for the station wagon. Someone has to tip the thieves off where the dogs are located. An ice cream man who drives around the neighborhood would be perfect."

"Then let's check them both out." Maryellen tried to sip the last of her float, but sadness crept over her and she couldn't finish it. Was Scooter trapped in Mr. Brad's apartment? Or locked up at Bark Haven? Either way, he'd be so lonely without her and the rest of the Larkins.

"We gotta fly though." Wayne checked his wrist, making sure the other two saw that he was wearing a snazzy new Superman watch. "Mom expects me home in an hour."

Ten minutes later, the three reached the apartment house just in time to see Mr. Brad coming out the front door with a cute little white terrier on a green leash. When he went down the steps and saw them, he waved jauntily. "Hi kids!" he called, before turning to walk in the other direction.

Maryellen stared after Mr. Brad and his dog until the two disappeared around the corner. Mr. Brad sure didn't act like a criminal with something to hide. And it looked as if he had been telling the truth about his Westie *and* the tan station wagon. Were they totally wrong about him? Mayellen glanced at Davy.

"That only tells us he isn't taking Scooter or Buster for a walk," Davy said, as if he could read her mind.

"And that he's sure a good actor if he *is* part of a dognapping ring," Wayne added. "I vote we go to Bark Haven and talk to Miss Hopkins. We already know we can't get into Mr. Brad's apartment."

"We could wait until he comes back," Maryellen declared, but even as she said it, she knew that wasn't a good plan. If Mr. Brad was involved, he wouldn't tell them anything. Besides, they all had to get home soon, and she did want to go back to Bark Haven. As Davy had noted, it was odd that the station wagon had the same name as the rescue organization even if it wasn't spelled the same, and perhaps Miss Hopkins could clear up the difference.

But when the three kids rode down Sandy Lane to the Bark Haven building, the pickup truck was gone and the door was locked.

"Oh well, this will give us a chance to really look around," said Maryellen. She was disappointed not to find Miss Hopkins, but she couldn't help wondering if she'd missed Scooter the first time she'd looked. She peered in the front window, hoping to see her beloved dog staring back at her, but the office was dark inside and she couldn't see anything suspicious.

"Let's go back behind the building and take another look inside the dog pens," Davy said.

"Miss Hopkins may come back. You be the lookout, Wayne," Maryellen suggested.

"Why me?" Wayne protested.

"Because you're Sergeant Friday, and we're just the officers who do all the work," said Maryellen.

Wayne grinned and nodded.

"Whistle loudly if you see someone coming," Maryellen called as she and Davy ran around to the back. The dogs immediately burst into a chorus of barking.

"I don't think we'll hear Wayne if he does whistle," Davy shouted.

Maryellen checked all the pens, recognizing many of the dogs she'd seen earlier. None of the dogs wore collars, and some of them looked scruffy, as if they'd been strays for a while. Then she noticed a white dog peeking out shyly from the last kennel, its head low and its ears laid back. Right away Maryellen could see from the black spots on its white head that it was a Dalmatian.

She grabbed Davy's arm. "Look! That could be Spots, the Bateses' missing dog!"

chapter 8

Dogs in Demand

DAVY PEERED AT the shy dog. "What makes you think it's the Bateses' pet?" he asked Maryellen.

"I don't know for sure. But we can call the family and tell them about Bark Haven. I'm sure they'll recognize their own dog—and Spots will recognize them. If it is him."

"Even if it isn't their dog, I'd say we found lots of evidence today," Davy said. "I know you're feeling discouraged that we didn't find Scooter. I could tell by the way you didn't finish your root beer float."

"I *am* discouraged." Maryellen heaved a sigh. "But you're right—we learned so much today that it will take up two whole pages in my notebook. And we have several important things to report to Officer Polansky. Maybe with our information the police will do something." Maryellen told the dogs good-bye, and then she and Davy hurried to the front of the building.

There was no Wayne waiting for them.

"So much for our lookout," Davy grumbled. "Though I need to get home, too."

"And I need to call Officer Polansky and the Bateses."

The moment they got home, Maryellen dashed inside with Davy and dialed Mr. Bates to tell him about the Dalmatian at Bark Haven. "Please let me know if it is Spots," she added before hanging up.

Feeling braver about talking to the police, she dialed them next. Officer Polansky wasn't on duty, so she gave another policeman her name and phone number. "Make sure he calls me, please," she said.

"Well?" Davy asked after she had hung up.

"That officer acted like I was a crank caller asking 'Is your refrigerator running?'"

"Then you'd better catch it," Davy finished the

joke. "Well, Sergeant, I've gotta be going, too. See you at school tomorrow."

Maryellen was alone in the house. With so many siblings, this was a rare occurrence, and after her busy day she relished the peace and quiet. She wandered into the kitchen, opened the refrigerator, and stared inside. Her mom had made Jell-O salad and Jell-O pudding, and there were hamburger patties ready to be grilled. Just then the phone rang. Maryellen picked it up, hoping it was Officer Polansky.

"Hi sweetie, I'm calling from the drugstore. We're picking up some lotion for the boys," her mother said. "We'll be home soon. Will you make a salad, please?" Before Maryellen could answer, she heard the pharmacist talking in the background, and her mother bid a hasty good-bye.

Maryellen hung up the phone and went back to

the refrigerator, pulling out lettuce, celery, and carrots. When she opened the cupboard where the big salad bowl was kept, she counted ten boxes of Jell-O, each with a square hole in it where Maryellen had cut out a contest entry form. While she chopped carrots and celery and washed and tore lettuce leaves, she tried to come up with a prize-winning jingle, hoping it would keep her from missing Scooter. But the house was too quiet.

Maryellen glanced around. The sun was beginning to set, and shadows darkened the kitchen. A shiver sent goose bumps up her arms. Being alone felt strange. Scooter had *always* been there. Without him, the house seemed extra empty and lonely.

Just then she heard her father call out a cheerful hello as he came in through the front door and switched on a light. Quickly, she tucked the finished salad into the refrigerator and ran into the living room. She was so glad to see him and feeling so lost without Scooter that she gave him a huge hug. He loosened his tie, set down his briefcase, and gave her a big hug right back. After she told him everything, he took his car keys from his pants pocket. "It's time we talked to the police in person," he said. "Leave your mom a note so she knows where we're going and that we'll be late for dinner."

The Daytona Beach Police Station was on Main Street. The building was slightly bigger than the Larkins' house, but the tall cement columns flanking its entrance, and the high counter just inside the door, made Maryellen feel unexpectedly small. She was relieved to find Officer Polansky on duty, sitting at a desk covered with folders and candy wrappers. He was tall, with a kind face that immediately set her at ease. After Maryellen told him about Bark Haven and Barkhaven, he frowned.

"Bark Haven is licensed by the city to pick up stray dogs and find them homes," he told Maryellen and her father. "The police also take strays there. We've never had a complaint about Miss Hopkins or the organization."

"I'm not complaining," Maryellen said. "I'm just wondering why the Barkhaven station wagon was trying to lure a dog into the vehicle, when it was obviously someone's pet."

"Good question. Right now, the city doesn't have the resources to investigate stolen, lost, or runaway dogs." He sighed. "It's just not a priority. I'm sorry."

"I'm sorry, too." Maryellen felt defeated once again. Her father squeezed her shoulder encouragingly.

"I hope the officers will at least keep their eyes out for this Barkhaven station wagon," she went on. "Oh, I almost forgot the most important information! My friend Davy got the license plate number." Maryellen gave the officer the number, which he wrote in his own notebook.

He smiled at her. "Good detective work, Miss

Larkin. This will help us track down the station wagon. Be aware, though, that the laws concerning stolen animals are very lax. Rarely are animal thiefs caught or convicted."

Maryellen's eyes widened. "Why?"

He shrugged. "Dogs aren't considered valuable property like money or jewelry. And it's hard to prove a dog was forcibly taken and didn't just run away."

"That's terrible!" Maryellen said. No wonder it was so easy for someone to steal a dog. A thief could safely assume he would never be caught!

"Still, I hope the police will act quickly," Mr. Larkin said, sounding serious. "We don't want strange men driving around our neighborhoods. They may be stealing other things besides dogs."

"I agree," Officer Polansky said. "And I will inform the officers who patrol The Palms about the station wagon and give them the license plate number." He smiled at Maryellen. "I'm a dog lover myself, so I've been doing some investigating on my own. And it seems that more dogs are missing than the few who tend to stray off or get lost."

"You suspect someone is taking them?" Maryellen asked. "But why would someone steal a dog?"

"What I'm reading in our police bulletins is that hospitals and science and medical labs are using more animals for research, so dogs are in demand now," the officer explained. "Most labs get their dogs from licensed dealers. Those are professional kennel owners who raise dogs to sell and are inspected and approved by the state."

Maryellen shuddered at the thought of dogs like Scooter being used for experiments.

"Lately, though, the bulletins report that more and more unlicensed dealers are springing up," Officer Polansky continued. "They steal pets and sell them to labs cheaper than the labs can buy them from the official dealers. This is illegal, but most police departments—like ours—don't have the manpower to go after these unscrupulous people."

"Wow, so there really are dognappers," Maryellen said. "Do you think the real Bark Haven is selling stolen dogs to labs?"

"I hope not. When I find the time, I will check out that organization again." He smiled at Maryellen. "And I will definitely keep watch for a portly dachshund."

"Thank you, Officer Polanksy." Maryellen and Mr. Larkin shook hands with him. She was glad he was on the case. And she'd learned something new—and frightening. If dogs were being used in experiments for science and medicine, that could explain why someone would steal *her* dog.

"Dad, we *have* to find Scooter," she burst out when they reached the car. "If he has been sold to a lab, he could be in even more trouble than we thought."

"I agree. Now that we know there are real thieves targeting animals, the situation's gotten more serious. Fortunately, it sounds as if Officer Polansky is investigating the missing dogs in the city as well."

"That's good, because our investigation could really use another detective. So far, nothing we've done has gotten us very far."

Mr. Larkin held open the car door for her. "I know I haven't been much help, but I love Scooter, and I'm on the case now, too. I'll do whatever I can to help."

"Thanks, Dad." With all her heart, Maryellen hoped it would make a difference.

The next day at school, Maryellen's brain was so awhirl with questions that she couldn't concentrate on Miss Deeny, her science teacher.

Now she knew the reason why dogs were stolen—they were used in labs, so they were worth money to thieves. Bark Haven would be the perfect way for dog thieves to hide what they were really up to, Maryellen realized. The organization was even licensed by the city!

Had Scooter been lured into the Barkhaven station wagon? Were Bark Haven and Miss Hopkins involved? Was she pretending to rescue dogs only to sell them? Was that why Miss Hopkins was so nervous when they wanted to see the kennels—because there were stolen dogs in the kennels? Maybe Scooter had even been inside the building somewhere, and when Maryellen, Davy, and Wayne had left, Miss Hopkins had quickly taken him to a laboratory and sold him.

"It is not confirmed, but the Soviet Union is experimenting with sending dogs into space," Miss Deeny said.

The word "dogs" penetrated Maryellen's jumbled mind. Sitting straighter in her seat, she focused on what the teacher was saying.

"The race to send rockets and satellites into space is heating up," Miss Deeny went on as she pointed to a map. "Currently the Soviet Union is ahead of the United States. Rumor is spreading that they have sent dogs one hundred kilometers into the air. "

Davy's hand went up. "How high is a hundred kilometers?"

"That's sixty-two miles. Almost the distance between Daytona Beach and Saint Augustine."

"Do the dogs wear tiny space suits?" another student asked.

Miss Deeny shook her head. "Because the Soviet Union has not released official statements on sending dogs into space, we don't know details."

Dogs in space! Maryellen's eyes widened. She couldn't believe what she was hearing!

"Cape Canaveral, a military base right near us here in Florida, is a missile range experimenting with rockets," Miss Deeny added. "It has launched several already, including one that flew fifty-five miles. But the point I'm trying to make is that the United States needs young scientists like you to help our country beat the Soviet Union, which brings me to your science report topics."

Maryellen tuned her teacher out as a hurricane of ideas spun through her head. Cape Canaveral was close to Daytona Beach. Miss Deeny said it was a missile range sending rockets into space. What if the United States was using dogs for its space program, too? What if Miss Hopkins sold Scooter to the military base?

Maryellen pictured the dachshund with a big bubble-shaped helmet on his head like the space suits from *Destination Moon*, an old movie she'd seen at the cinema. She gasped out loud—right now, Scooter could be in training for a trip into outer space!

chapter 9

Lost in Space?

MARYELLEN CLAPPED HER hand over her mouth, stifling the gasp. Davy shot her a funny look. Maybe it was a wild hunch, but still Maryellen shuddered at the thought of her chubby dachshund being strapped into a rocket and shot into space.

Though he *would* be famous, she suddenly realized. She imagined the two of them in a parade like the one she'd been in on Memorial Day. They'd ride in the mayor's convertible; Scooter would wear his space helmet, and she'd wear a new dress with patriotic stars and stripes.

Maryellen loved fame. But she loved Scooter more. She didn't want him blasting to the moon in a rocket. She wanted him *home*.

"Maryellen? Your topic?" Miss Deeny asked.

"Cape Canaveral," Maryellen said quickly.

Miss Deeny nodded. "A great choice."

A *really* great choice if you are hunting for your missing dog, Maryellen wanted to add, but she held her tongue. Her father had said he would help. Would he take her to Cape Canaveral so she could find information for her report—and search for Scooter the space dog?

That afternoon, when her father came home from work, he listened patiently while she explained about Scooter possibly being sold to Cape Canaveral. "I know it's kind of a wild idea," she added quickly. "That's why I also chose the missile range for my science report." She hesitated, then asked, "Will you take me there tomorrow? It's Saturday. Please?"

Her father thought for a moment. "Only if you get permission for a visit. It's not a tourist attraction like Cypress Gardens, so the range may not give tours."

"I'll tell them I am a young scientist who wants to help America win the race into space." She jabbed her finger in the air to make her point.

Her father laughed. "That should convince them. I have an Air Force buddy who may be able to get me the phone number. I doubt they're in the phone book."

Maryellen gave him a big hug. "Thanks, Dad. May I invite Davy, too?"

"Sure, kiddo."

She hurried over to the Fenstermachers' house and found Davy on the front lawn tossing a baseball in the air and catching it. As soon as she mentioned a trip to Cape Canaveral, he got excited. "Maybe I can even learn something for my science report."

"I'm going for my own report, but mostly because I think Miss Hopkins sold Scooter to some place that uses dogs for experiments." Maryellen filled Davy in on all she'd learned from Officer Polansky. "And you heard Miss Deeny say the Russians are training dogs for outer space. Well, what if Cape Canaveral is using dogs in its space program? I mean, think about it: A dog shaped like a hot dog with short, stubby legs is just what the scientists need to fit in a rocket."

"By golly, Sergeant Friday, I think you're on to something." Davy mimicked Officer Smith's voice from *Dragnet*.

Maryellen grinned. "So will you come with us tomorrow? If we get permission for a tour?"

"I wouldn't miss it for anything."

"I can't believe you called an Air Force base and talked to a real soldier," Carolyn said later that night. She was using cold cream to wipe off the mascara on her lashes. She'd had a second date with Dreamy Drew after school. Then Dreamy Drew had helped Carolyn and Maryellen babysit while Mr. and Mrs. Larkin went out to dinner with friends. Drew had lasted through roller skating in the driveway, Chinese checkers, and a round of Go Fish before leaving.

Tom and Mikey were so tuckered out they'd fallen asleep right away. Beverly had read for two minutes before falling asleep, too, even though the bedroom light was on. Maryellen was allowed to stay up until her parents came home. It made her feel grown up.

"His name is Lieutenant Jenkins," Maryellen told Carolyn. "He was very nice. He said we wouldn't be allowed to go in any restricted areas, though. Which is where Scooter might be," she added glumly. "Why don't you come tomorrow? You can help me snoop around. I need another shrewd detective on this case." Maryellen pulled her notebook from under her pillow and read all the clues to her big sister. It never hurt to get someone else's opinion.

"Wow, you've done a lot of investigating. After listening to all you've discovered, I think you're right: Scooter was stolen." Carolyn frowned. "It's really scary to think that thieves are here right in our neighborhood." She set down her hairbrush and turned to face Maryellen. "Did you hear from Officer Polansky about who owns the station wagon? The police need to track down those creeps."

"No. He said he sent a teletype to the state's motor vehicle office and hopes to hear back soon."

Just then the phone rang. Beverly turned in her sleep and mumbled. "I'll get it," Maryellen told Carolyn as she rushed down the hall. She hoped it was Officer Polansky.

It turned out to be Mr. Bates, the owner of Spots, the missing Dalmatian.

"Did you find him?" Maryellen asked breathlessly.

"No." Mr. Bates sounded sad. "We checked at Bark Haven. The organization did pick up a Dalmatian, but it isn't Spots. Our dog has a funny black ring around his right eye, and this one doesn't. And it has been there almost four weeks."

"So you saw the other Dalmatian?"

"Yes. The volunteer we spoke with said that after a dog has been at the organization for over a month, it usually gets sent somewhere else, but fortunately, this dog is going to be adopted by a family. Anyway, thank you for telling us about the place. The volunteer took down all our information in case Spots does show up there."

"We'll keep our eyes open for Spots, too," said Maryellen. Mr. Bates hung up, and she bounded back down the hall to tell Carolyn the news. Suddenly she remembered what Mr. Bates had also said: *Dogs that have been at the organization for over a month are sent somewhere else.*

Was that "somewhere else" the lab at Cape Canaveral where dogs were used for experiments? She couldn't wait to go to the range and confront the soldiers and scientists who worked there.

She'd march right up to them as if she were Nancy Drew. She'd whip out her notebook and interrogate them with steely eyes. This time, she was coming home with answers *and* her dog.

chapter 10

Top Secret!

"NEW YORK," DAVY called out. A second later, Maryellen hollered, "Georgia!"

The drive to Cape Canaveral took over an hour, so Davy and Maryellen amused themselves finding license plates from different states. Florida attracted a lot of tourists, so it wasn't hard to find states from far away. The two sat in the backseat of Mr. Larkin's Chevy, while Carolyn sat in the front. Even Carolyn got excited when she saw a Maine plate.

Looking at license plates reminded Maryellen that Officer Polansky still hadn't called. "I hope the police haven't given up finding the Barkhaven station wagon," she said to Davy with a sigh.

"He's probably busy solving a jewelry store robbery," Davy said.

Maryellen wrinkled her nose. "Jewelry isn't as important as Scooter." She picked up one of the copies of *Popular Science* magazine she'd asked Davy to bring along. Before they left, Maryellen had tried to think up questions to ask Lieutenant Jenkins, but she was having a hard time. If she couldn't even ask intelligent questions about rockets, how was she going to interrogate him about Scooter?

The only thing she knew about the space race was what she'd learned during the summer Science Club when the teams had to invent a flying machine. And Cape Canaveral was so new it wasn't even an entry in the school's encyclopedia.

"Help me find an article on rockets," she said to Davy.

"And you help me find some information about communication in outer space," he said, as the two of them began flipping through the pages. There were pictures of a glider that flew thirteen miles and a mobile trash burner, but Maryellen didn't see anything about rockets or space communication.

Mr. Larkin looked at Maryellen in the rearview mirror. "When we get there, you'll want to listen, observe, and take notes. Did you bring something to write on?"

Maryellen held up her notebook. She'd decided to add Cape Canaveral information to the clues about Scooter, though on separate pages.

"I did, too." Carolyn held up a pad and pen. "I'm on the case."

"I brought my camera," Mr. Larkin added. "I'm on the case, too."

"And I brought licorice," Davy chimed in, shaking a candy box. "So I am definitely on the case."

They turned off Highway 1 and drove east on a two-lane road past motels, beach houses, orange groves, and a trailer park. Maryellen looked out the window as they crossed several bridges that spanned marshes. Soon there were no more buildings, only water and marsh grass.

Finally they passed a sign: **Cape Canaveral Missile Test Annex. Patrick Air Force Base.** Maryellen sat up so she could look out the front windshield. The car passed a high tower built of steel girders that cast a long shadow on the ground. Near the tower was an igloo-shaped structure with a recessed door.

Everyone was silent as they stared out the windows. "Wow," Carolyn finally said. "Have we landed on the moon?"

"This is definitely like something from a movie," agreed Davy.

All Maryellen could think about was how lonely Scooter must be with no family to play with or pet him.

As they drove east, they reached a black-and-white lighthouse that rose into the sky. Several identical clapboard buildings with porches were clustered around it. Each had a sign in front.

"Lieutenant Jenkins said to meet him in front of

the building that said 'Patrick Air Force Base Support
Office,'" Maryellen said.

As Mr. Larkin parked the car, a handsome young
man in uniform hurried down the steps. "Oooh, he's
cute," Carolyn whispered.

"Miss Maryellen Larkin?" the officer asked as the
four got out of the car. "I'm Lieutenant Jenkins and
will be your family's guide this morning."

"Nice to meet you!" Maryellen shook hands with
him. Mr. Larkin introduced himself and then Carolyn
and Davy.

"Welcome to Patrick Air Force Base, also known
as Cape Canaveral," Lieutenant Jenkins continued.
"As I told you on the phone, most of the base is
restricted to Army, Air Force, and official person-
nel, but I can show you enough for you to write your
school report. The U.S. military is always happy to
educate young minds."

"Thank you, sir. I mean officer. I mean
L-Lieutenant," Maryellen stammered. She saluted

him to cover her awkwardness and then immediately felt silly.

He saluted her back and smiled. "You can call me Lieutenant. Follow me and we'll get the tour started."

Clutching her pencil and notebook, Maryellen hurried after him along with Carolyn, Davy, and Dad. The lieutenant led them to an old Jeep with an open top. The three kids squeezed into the back and sat on the hard bench seat, and Mr. Larkin sat in front. Lieutenant Jenkins zipped down a lane, gravel and sand flying, toward a tower similar to the one they had passed on their way into the range.

"This is Launch Pad 3, once used for testing Air Force winged missiles," Lieutenant Jenkins hollered over the rumble of the motor. Maryellen tried to write in her notebook, but each bounce caused her words to jiggle across the page.

"In 1950, the first rocket, called Bumper 8, was launched from Cape Canaveral right on this spot." He wheeled the Jeep around the concrete base of the steel tower. All the kids had to crane their necks to see the top. "The steel frame is an old gantry," Lieutenant Jenkins went on. "It was a tower used to launch missiles. Underneath the tower and the concrete are underground tunnels that lead to power generators."

"How high in the sky did Bumper 8 go?" Davy asked.

"Did it go all the way to outer space?" Maryellen chimed in. She swallowed hard as she imagined a dog strapped into Bumper 8, hurtling through the air.

"Not quite." Lieutenant Jenkins laughed. "It went about a hundred and fifty miles over the Atlantic. A Navy ship tracked it before it plunged into the water."

"Oh." Maryellen's shoulders slumped. She doubted the Air Force would send a dog straight into the ocean.

"Since then we've sent missiles higher and farther. Not to the moon or Mars, though."

The lieutenant parked the Jeep. Maryellen, Davy, and Carolyn continued to ask questions while

Mr. Larkin shot some photos. Then the lieutenant drove them to one of the structures that looked like igloos. "This is a blockhouse, built to protect the launch crew in case the rocket blows up," he explained.

Maryellen shuddered, hoping no animals were involved.

"Have any blown up?" Carolyn asked.

"Bumper 7 misfired on the launchpad but didn't explode. Back then there was only a wooden block-house. It would not have offered much protection if there had been an explosion."

"Can we go inside the blockhouse?" Maryellen asked hopefully. So far there was no sign of a build-ing to house dogs.

"No. It contains top-secret scientific instruments. Sorry."

Top-secret scientific instruments! That sounded important, Maryellen thought. And maybe those instruments were used for experimenting on dogs!

"Now if there aren't any more questions, I'll take

you back to your car," said Lieutenant Jenkins.

Maryellen took a deep breath. She couldn't wait any longer to ask about Scooter. "Our science teacher said that the Russians are sending dogs into space. Is Cape Canaveral training dogs to fly in its rockets?"

The lieutenant shook his head. "Right now, the Soviets are ahead of us in the race to space. But we are catching up. President Eisenhower is pouring money and resources into new technology. One day, we hope to send a man into orbit."

"Not a dog?" Maryellen persisted.

Lieutenant Jenkins gave her a puzzled look.

"Excuse my sister, Lieutenant," Carolyn spoke up. "Our dog Scooter is missing, and the Daytona Beach Police told us someone is stealing dogs in the city, probably to sell for use as test animals."

"And Scooter is the perfect size to fit in a rocket," Davy added.

"So that's why the questions about dogs in space," Lieutenant Jenkins said. "I'm sorry about your missing dog, but I can assure you that no animals are here on the Cape except for seagulls and mosquitoes. The Soviets may be using dogs, but right now the United States is concentrating on sending unmanned rockets into orbit."

Maryellen didn't know whether she felt happy or sad. She was glad that Scooter wasn't going to be shot into space, but she was sad that this trip had turned out to be one more dead end.

"I know that doesn't help you find your dog," Lieutenant Jenkins said. "Animals are sold to pharmaceutical laboratories, though. Some are used to test the ingredients and chemicals in medicines and other products to make sure they are safe for humans."

"Thank you so much for the tour," Mr. Larkin said. "Maryellen learned enough here to get an A on her report about the missile range."

"Yes, thank you very much." Maryellen shook hands with Lieutenant Jenkins.

The lieutenant dropped them off at their car,

and Maryellen slid into the backseat with Davy. She opened her notebook, trying to remember all that she had learned. "I can't believe we didn't find Scooter here," she said. "I feel like the trip was a waste of time."

Immediately Carolyn turned around in the front seat. "Why, Maryellen Larkin! You learned a lot on this trip. Being a detective means ruling out suspects, and you just ruled out a major one."

"Plus you'll get an A on your report for sure," Davy said. "That place was awesome. I bet no other kid in Florida—why, in the whole world—has been there."

"How's that going to help me find Scooter?"

"You also learned more about pharmaceutical companies using dogs to test ingredients in products and medicines," Mr. Larkin pointed out.

"True, that adds to what Officer Polansky said about labs using dogs for experiments," Maryellen said, feeling a little better. "Are there any of those kinds of companies around Daytona Beach?"

"Let's look in the phone book when we get home," suggested Dad.

"We can also go back and talk to Miss Hopkins," Davy said. "I bet she knows more than she's letting on."

"Like where all the stray, lost, and *stolen* dogs end up," Carolyn said.

"You guys are right. Sorry I was such a Gloomy Gus." Maryellen smiled. "As soon as I get home, I'm calling the police station. Maybe by now Officer Polansky has found the dognappers who own the station wagon and made an arrest!

chapter 11

Friends to the Rescue

MRS. LARKIN, BEVERLY, Tom, and Mikey came running out the front door when the Chevy pulled into the driveway. Davy grabbed his magazines, said a quick good-bye, and headed to his house.

"How was the trip?" Mrs. Larkin asked when the others climbed from the car. "Did you get some interesting information for your science report, Ellie?"

"Did you see rockets blow up?" Tom asked.

"Did you find Scooter?" Beverly chimed in.

"Did you bring me a present?" Mikey tugged on Maryellen's shirt hem.

"Goodness, you would think we'd been gone for a week instead of for a morning," Carolyn said. "Did Drew call?"

"Yes, he called . . ." Mrs. Larkin replied, but Carolyn was already rushing into the house. "And Officer Polansky called as well."

Maryellen gasped. "What did he say? Did he find the thieves and Scooter?"

Her mother shook her head. "The license plate came back to a vehicle stolen over a month ago in Miami. So they can't trace the driver."

"That's terrible!" Maryellen sagged against the car door. She felt as if someone had punched her in the stomach.

"Not totally terrible," said Mrs. Larkin. "Officer Polansky says that because the car is stolen, it will get more attention from the police. Still, I'm sorry the news isn't better, sweetie."

"I was counting on Officer Polansky. Now we'll never find Scooter." Maryellen could feel her lips quivering. She knew she was acting like a big baby, but she didn't care.

Suddenly Mikey burst into tears. "Now we'll

nevew find Scootew," he echoed.

Mr. Larkin gave his wife a kiss. "Sorry you had to be the one to break the bad news. Guys, I think Maryellen needs time to pull herself together. Come on, let's go inside. I did bring presents."

"What? What?" Beverly, Mikey, and Tom crowded around their father as he walked with Mrs. Larkin into the house.

"They're special space rocks from Launch Pad 3. . . ."

Maryellen stood in the middle of the driveway, willing herself not to cry. Her hopes had been sky high, and now they had crashed to the ground. She'd been counting on Officer Polansky to find that car, which would lead her to Scooter. That was her mistake, she realized as she dragged herself up the sidewalk and plopped on the front step. She needed to count on herself, not the police.

It was still early. She could ride to Bark Haven right now. Or she could ride around the neighborhood until she found the station wagon again.

Oh, who was she kidding? She couldn't do it
herself. And right now she didn't have the energy to
gather a detective team together.

Mrs. Larkin came out of the house and sat on the
steps with her. "Sorry, sweetie." She rocked sideways and gently bumped shoulders with Maryellen.
"You've been working so hard to find Scooter. I know
you're disappointed."

"It's been almost a week that he's been gone."
Maryellen's eyes welled. "I just miss him so much,
and I'm worried about him." She leaned into her
mother, who put her arm around her and held her
close. Maryellen couldn't hold back the tears.

"I miss him, too. We all do," said Mom. "Scooter
is part of our family." She handed Maryellen a hand-
kerchief embroidered with tiny pink flowers. "This
belonged to my mother, who got it from her mother.
It's dried a lot of tears and sniffles."

"Thanks." Maryellen hiccupped.

Mom smiled. "While you were out, someone else

called, too. Actually three someones."

"Three people? Who?"

"Karen, Karen, and Angela. They have a surprise for you."

"A surprise?" Maryellen swallowed. "Oh, Mom, I don't know if I can face them and their chattering."

"You'll have to, because they'll be here any minute. I told them you would be home about lunchtime. I think they may just cheer you up."

"The only thing that will cheer me up is finding Scooter."

Just then Karen King's father pulled up in his car. Maryellen's three friends burst from the backseat, dragging large pieces of white paper and a picnic basket. Quickly, Maryellen wiped her eyes.

"We're here to help find Scooter!" Angela said.

"We've named ourselves the Critter Rescue Club," Karen Stohlman added. She held up one of the large pieces of paper, which Maryellen could see was poster board. A picture of a brown dog with a pointy nose, floppy ears, and and a long body was drawn on it. "We made ten of these to put up in the neighborhood."

"Look, it says—" Karen King ran her finger across the top and bottom of the poster as she read, "Lost Dog Scooter. Please call DA-3490 if found. Reward."

"These are great," Maryellen said even though the drawing on the posters looked more like a sausage than a dog. "What's the reward?"

Angela pulled out a wallet from her purse. "We put all our allowances together. We have 75 cents."

"Wow. Thank you. I can add 25 cents to that to make a dollar." Maryellen grinned. Her mother was right—her friends had made her feel better. Even though it seemed more and more certain that Scooter had not wandered off or run away, offering a reward couldn't hurt.

Angela held up the picnic basket. "We made lunch, too. Tuna sandwiches and chips."

"We figure we'll get hungry hammering all these

signs up," Karen King added. "Can we borrow hammers and nails?"

"Sure. My dad's tools are in the carport," said Maryellen.

"Let's get to work," Karen Stohlman said.

"I think we should eat first," Angela said. "Before the tuna goes bad."

"I agree—Maryellen needs a pick-me-up," Karen Stohlman chimed in. "She looks as if she's in 'the depths of despair.' I learned that from reading *Anne of Green Gables*."

Karen King held up a poster. "Work first. Getting these posters up will raise her spirits. Then we'll eat."

"By then the bread will be soggy," Angela said.

"It's three against one," Karen Stohlman said to the other Karen. "Right, Maryellen? I'm counting you on my side."

Maryellen put her fingers in her ears. "Stop! No more arguing. Remember what happened last time?"

The three shut their mouths.

"Let's put up half the posters, then eat," Maryellen said. "If we walk down this street, we'll end at the playground, where there's a picnic table. I am hungry, but we need to get these posters hung so people playing outside today can see them. All right?"

All three nodded. "We won't let you down this time," Karen King said. "We even came up with our own jingle. Listen!" And all three girls chorused,

> *Skinny or fat,*
> *Snake or cat*
> *Large or small,*
> *We'll find them all.*
> *Critter Rescue Club is on the case!*

Maryellen burst out laughing. Mom was right. Her friends had *definitely* made her feel better.

The four gathered up the posters, the hammers, the nails, and the picnic basket. Working together, they tacked posters on telephone poles at each end of several blocks. By then they had reached the playground, and Maryellen's stomach was rumbling with hunger.

While they ate at a picnic table under a tree, Maryellen told her friends about the trip to Cape Canaveral. She didn't mention anything about looking for Scooter there. So far, the Karens and Angela still thought the dachshund had simply wandered off.

"Lieutenant Jenkins was so handsome, he swept Carolyn off her feet," she said, finishing her story with a romantic twist.

"Isn't she dating Drew Mancini?" Karen King asked.

"She's not serious about him." Maryellen took a bite. "She's playing the field. She's not like Joan, who dated Jerry for forever and then married him."

The conversation drifted to Joan's wedding, which the four had fun discussing. Joan had gotten married in the Larkins' backyard. Carolyn had played the wedding march on the piano, and Maryellen had been a bridesmaid.

"Did you know Tom was going to sing, 'Here comes the bride, all dressed in white, stepped on a turtle and down fell her girdle?'" Maryellen told them as her three friends laughed. "Fortunately, my mom stopped him just in time."

After that, talk switched to Maryellen getting her picture in the *Daytona Beach News Journal* last summer because she'd ridden in the parade.

"Everyone in the world recognized you, didn't they?" Karen King said. "You were famous."

"Fame sure is fleeting," Karen Stohlman remarked.

Suddenly Angela clapped her hands. "That's it! We should get a picture of Scooter in the newspaper!"

"Wow, Angela, great idea," Karen King said. "I wish I'd thought of it. Everyone in Daytona Beach would be on the lookout for him."

"But Scooter's not famous," Karen Stohlman said. "Why would the newspaper print a photo of him?"

Maryellen's eyes widened as she listened. Now she knew her next step—maybe the police would put more effort into investigating a rash of missing dogs if the newspaper printed an article. All she had to do was tell a reporter what she'd learned about thieves stealing dogs for use in labs.

She gave Angela a hug. "What a fabulous idea! Let's hurry and finish lunch. Critter Rescue Club, we have news to report!"

chapter 12

A Frustrating Witness

"WHILE WE'RE EATING, I have something to tell you." Maryellen took her notebook from her pocket. By the time she had finished informing Karen, Karen, and Angela about what *really* might have happened to Scooter, the three had stopped chewing and were staring at her in horror.

"Stolen?" Karen Stohlman gasped. "By dog-nappers?"

Karen King shuddered. "That sounds like something out of a TV show!"

"I had no idea companies were using animals and experimenting on them like lab rats," Angela said.

"A rat is an animal," Karen Stohlman pointed out.

"You know what I mean," said Angela.

"The plot thickens," Karen King announced in a

dramatic voice. "The Critter Rescue Club really has a job to do now."

"Do you think we have enough information to get a *News Journal* reporter to write an article for the paper?" Angela asked.

"I hope so." Maryellen closed her notebook. "And if the newspaper isn't interested, we can write a letter to the editor. Joan wrote one when she was in high school about trash on the beach, which got lots of attention."

The four friends hurried through lunch, chattering excitedly about what to tell a reporter. Then they headed from the playground to hang more posters, splitting up so they could go faster. The Karens were eager to get started writing a newspaper story, "Daytona Dognappers Take Over the City" (Karen K.) or "Dog Thieves Leave Owners in Depths of Despair" (Karen S.).

Maryellen and Angela were hammering a poster on a pole in front of the swing set when two girls looked up from the hopscotch game they had been playing on the sidewalk. When they saw what Maryellen and the other Critter Rescuers were doing, they hurried over.

"Our dog is missing, too," the oldest one said. She had ribbon-tied pigtails, and Maryellen recognized her from school.

"You're Junie Pursley, right?" Maryellen said. "You're in the same grade as my sister, Beverly."

"Yeah, and this is my little sister, Suzanne." Suzanne smiled. She had no front teeth. "She's in first grade."

"When did your dog go missing?" Maryellen asked, pulling out her notebook and frowning at the news that a fourth dog had disappeared.

"Five days ago in the afternoon. I've been keeping track."

That was when Scooter had gone missing! Maryellen realized with a start. "Had the ice cream truck just come by?"

"No. He came later on. Suzanne was out in the yard with our dog when he disappeared."

A witness! Maryellen turned her attention to the little girl. "Did you see a station wagon with a sign that said Barkhaven?"

Suzanne shrugged her skinny shoulders. "I'm just learning to read."

A frustrating witness.

"What's your dog's name and description?"

"He's a beagle with black and brown spots," Junie said. "We named him Jumper 'cause . . ."

"He lovthe to jump," Suzanne said with a lisp. Maryellen wrote furiously. Angela squatted in front of the little girl. "Suzanne, tell us *exactly* what happened the day Jumper went missing."

The little girl screwed up her face, thinking hard. "Wel-l-l-l, I got up in the morning and watched TV before school."

"No, I mean when Jumper disappeared," Angela clarified.

"Wel-l-l, me and Jumper were digging in the mud waiting for Junie when a car thtopped in front of the houthe. A man opened the door and called, 'Here boy, come get a treat.' Jumper jumped in the car and they left, and I thtarted to cry."

Maryellen couldn't believe her ears. It had to be the same dognappers who tried to lure the collie into the car—and probably took Scooter!

Suzanne began to snuffle. Angela patted her shoulder. "It's okay. We're the Critter Rescue Club. We'll help you find Jumper."

Maryellen asked Junie for the family's address and phone number.

"We live there." She pointed to a pink house directly across from the playground. Maryellen wrote down the street and number. Junie knew her phone number, and Maryellen wrote it down, too. Then the two girls wandered back to their hopscotch game.

"I wonder how many more dogs have gone missing," she mused as she closed her notepad. "So far, that's four for sure: Scooter, Jumper, Misty, Spots, and maybe Buster."

"It is eerie," Angela said. "Poof, they vanished. All this stuff about stolen dogs going to laboratories is giving me the creeps." Angela shivered. "I'm keeping Amerigo on a leash from now on."

"Good idea." Maryellen put the last nail in her poster, then she and Angela met back up with the Karens and told them about the missing beagle.

"I think we have more than enough to tell a reporter," said Karen Stohlman. "Let's go to the newspaper office right now."

"It's on the other side of town," Maryellen said. "We'd have to take the bus or get someone to drive us."

"My mom won't let me take the bus without a grown-up," Karen King said.

"The office might not be open on Saturday anyway," Maryellen added. "So let's write down our information and mail it to them. That's how Joan sent in her editorial."

The four girls hurried back to the Larkins' house. Carolyn was in the bathroom getting ready for a date. The rest of the family was in the backyard playing kick-ball. The four girls huddled on Carolyn's bed, all talking at once. By the time they agreed on what to put in the letter, Mr. King had returned to pick them up.

Maryellen waved good-bye. Not only had her friends cheered her up, but they'd also gotten a lot accomplished. She headed down the hall to start writing the letter to send to the paper. She needed a punchy opening that would be sure to get the attention of whoever opened the letter at the *News Journal* office.

As Maryellen passed the bathroom door, Carolyn stepped out, a towel wrapped around her head. Her hair dried in natural waves—which made Maryellen envious—so all she had to do was bobby pin it in a few places.

Maryellen sat on the bed and balanced a clip-board with a sheet of paper on her crossed legs. She wrinkled her forehead, trying to remember how Joan had started her letter to the editor. Something like, "If the people of Daytona Beach don't act, soon our beaches will be covered with trash."

Maybe she could sort of copy her sister's words: "If the people of Daytona Beach don't act, soon there will be no more dogs to bark at the milkman."

No, that was silly.

"Tell me which would get your attention," she said to her sister. "I can begin with the facts: 'The Daytona Beach Police have received many calls about missing dogs.' Or I can begin more dramatically: 'Do you have a dog? Then check to see if it's missing.'"

She looked up when Carolyn didn't say anything. Her sister was carefully applying Pink Blush lipstick and couldn't talk. She blotted it with a tissue and then checked her reflection in the mirror.

Maryellen thought back to what Lieutenant Jenkins had said about animals being used to test the ingredients in products to make sure they were safe for humans. Did that include lipstick? She'd been wrong about Scooter's being taken to test a rocket, but could her dog have been stolen just so girls like Carolyn could look pretty? The thought of it made her queasy.

Suddenly the phone rang. "Will you get that?" Carolyn asked. "If it's Drew, tell him I'm almost ready. We're going roller skating, so I don't have to look too luscious," she added jokingly.

Maryellen leaped down the hall. She could hear talking and banging from the kitchen, which meant that kickball was over. "Hello, Maryellen Larkin speaking."

"Hi, Miss Larkin, this is Mrs. Julia Palmer. I live on Hibiscus Street in The Palms. I saw your poster, and that's why I'm calling."

Maryellen caught her breath. "You found Scooter?"

"No. I'm calling because I have a missing dog, too. Pinky, my poodle, disappeared yesterday, and I can't find her anywhere."

chapter 13

Two Rings

MARYELLEN COULDN'T BELIEVE it.
That made six dogs in the neighborhood that had
possibly disappeared. She bet the police had an even
longer list.

"I'm sorry about your poodle," Maryellen told the
caller. "I have been investigating missing dogs since
Scooter vanished and—"

"I called the police," Mrs. Palmer cut in, "but they
said Pinky was probably lost and would come home."

"Scooter hasn't come home for almost a week.
There have been other missing dogs from the neighborhood, too."

"Mr. Palmer and I are beside ourselves with grief
and worry. Pinky is our baby!"

"You need to call the police again and talk to

Officer Polansky. He's been very helpful. You also need to visit Bark Haven. It's a dog rescue organization." Maryellen hesitated a moment before adding, "Or at least it claims to be. Pinky might be there."

Maryellen gave her Bark Haven's phone number and address.

"We must find her," Mrs. Palmer said. "Pinky will simply die if she doesn't have her steak dinner and squeaky toys."

"Can you describe Pinky?" Maryellen asked.

"She's a white miniature poodle. She wears a pink collar and pink bow," Mrs. Palmer said.

That'll make her easy to spot, Maryellen thought.

"If you see her, please, please, *please* call me at DA-2511," Mrs. Palmer pleaded.

Maryellen jotted down the Palmers' information before hanging up, then checked the time on the hall clock. It was 4:30. An hour and a half before dinner. The letter could wait until tonight. While it was still daylight, she needed to do some more investigating.

The Barkhaven thieves were obviously targeting The Palms, so it was time for a stakeout. She hoped the Dragnet team wasn't busy with basketball.

She called Davy, but Mrs. Fenstermacher said he was at the school gym practicing. That meant Wayne was there, too. Maryellen hung up. She'd just have to bike alone through the neighborhood until she spotted the station wagon. This time she was following it to wherever it took the dogs.

She ran into the kitchen, where the family was washing up. Mikey had muddy knees, Tom had a bloody nose, Beverly had twigs in her hair, and Mr. Larkin's white T-shirt was ripped.

"Gosh, I thought you were playing kickball," Maryellen said, "not tackle football."

"It got a little wild," Mrs. Larkin said. The back of her pedal pushers was muddy. "If you're wondering, I slid into first base," she added with a laugh.

"Is it all right if I bike around the neighborhood?" Maryellen asked.

"No, it is not all right," her father said. "Your mom needs help with supper." Maryellen started to protest, but he gave her that stern look that said "no arguing."

Mr. Larkin herded the two boys from the kitchen. "Come on, tigers, you two need a bath."

"Beverly, wash your hands and peel potatoes for me," Mrs. Larkin said. "Maryellen, I need you to chop celery and carrots. The beef bone and stock have been simmering since this morning, so it's time to add the vegetables."

"Nancy Drew never had to help fix dinner," Maryellen muttered.

"That's because she was an only child and had a housekeeper to do the chores," Mrs. Larkin pointed out.

Maryellen sighed. So much for investigating today. Tomorrow was Sunday. Maybe after church she could get Davy and Wayne or the Critter Rescue Club to patrol the neighborhood with her. She doubted the dognappers took time off.

"I did receive some fun news today," Maryellen's

mother said as she pulled the vegetables from the crisper.

"What?" Beverly stood on a stool so she could reach the faucet to wash her hands.

"We won fifth place in the Schwinn contest."

"Fifth? That means we didn't win a bike," Maryellen said grumpily. "How is that fun news?" Once again, she realized she was being a big baby, and really, she'd almost forgotten about the contest since Scooter had disappeared. But boy oh boy, a new bike would have been nice. She would no longer be Sergeant Slowpoke.

"I though fifth place was pretty good," her mom said.

Beverly hopped off the stool. "What did we win?"

"Bells for your bikes. Five of them."

"Oh, goodie!" Beverly clapped her hands. "I've always wanted a bell. Now everyone will know I'm coming. *Ka-ching, ching, ching!*"

Maryellen shrugged. She couldn't get as excited

as Beverly about some dumb bike bells.

Nothing seemed to be going her way today.

"I thought I'd make some Jell-O pudding for dessert. *Again*." Mrs. Larkin smiled as she reached into the cupboard. "Don't look so gloomy, Ellie. We've won prizes in two contests, which has inspired me. The deadline for Jell-O entries is in a few days."

"Can I help with the jingle?" Beverly asked. "I'm learning about rhyming words in school."

Maryellen was about to say no when she glanced over at Beverly. Her little sister was expertly peeling potatoes, and she'd been good help hunting for Scooter.

"It sure would be fun to go to New York," Mrs. Larkin said.

"Can we all go?" Beverly asked.

"The grand prize is three days for the entire family," Mrs. Larkin said.

"I want to see the Statue of Liberty," Beverly declared. "Let's see, Jell-O rhymes with yellow, bellow, hello, cello . . ."

"I want to see a musical on Broadway," Maryellen said as she washed three carrots. "'Play your cello while eating Jell-O with your favorite fellow.'"

Speaking of favorite fellow, after dinner, she'd talk to Davy about sleuthing tomorrow. For now, she turned her brain to jingles. Once they found Scooter, a trip to New York would be exactly what she needed.

After dinner, Maryellen finished her letter to the *News Journal,* using the notes from her notebook. She read it to her mother, who suggested a few corrections, adding, "Your letter is very well written. I do think you can leave out 'depths of despair,' but if I were a reporter, I would jump on this story right away."

Her mother helped her address and stamp the envelope. Monday before school, Maryellen would put it in the mailbox, so hopefully it would get delivered to the newspaper office on Tuesday, which still seemed like a long way away when you were missing your pet.

Next, Maryellen went through the phone book trying to find pharmaceutical companies in the business listings. She checked under the *F*'s with no luck. Her father was reading a magazine when she went into the living room. Beverly, Tom, and Mikey were lying on the floor watching *People Are Funny* on TV. Usually Maryellen enjoyed the show, but tonight she had something more important on her mind.

"Sorry to bother you," she said to her father, "but I can't find pharmaceutical companies in the phonebook. I found fabric shops, farm equipment . . . "

"Look under *P-H*," he said.

"Oh, right, like 'pharmacy.'" Maryellen flipped through the pages. "There's no listing for 'Pharmaceuticals'."

"Probably because the companies that make and test medicines and other products don't sell directly to the public. You'd need to know the name of the specific business."

"How am I going to find out that?" She shut the phone book in frustration. "I keep getting these leads and not being able to do anything about them. I wish I was a grown-up."

"I know it's frustrating. Like not being allowed to go biking when it's almost dark outside, right?" he teased.

"Right." She perched on the edge of the chair. "I wanted to look for that station wagon before dinner."

"Which is exactly why I said no to riding around the neighborhood by yourself while these dog thieves are in the area. You need to let the police do their jobs and catch them. I don't want you in harm's way."

"The police seem to be too busy to worry about stolen animals." Maryellen sighed. "Can I search tomorrow if Davy and Wayne are with me? Or Angela and the Karens? Maybe I'll just invite Angela. She's got a cool head."

"Promise you'll come home and call the police if you see the station wagon?" Mr. Larkin asked.

"I promise," Maryellen told him.

The next day after church and a fast lunch, the Dragnet team plus Angela met in front of the Larkins' house with their bikes. Maryellen brought four of the bells that she and her mother had won in the Schwinn contest. She got a screwdriver from the carport so they could attach the bells to their handlebars. During church she'd remembered what Beverly had said about using her bike bell to let everyone know she was coming. Maybe the four friends could use the bells to talk to each other, too. When she pushed the lever and heard the loud *ka-ching, ching,* she smiled. Not a bad prize after all!

"Pretty spiffy, Sergeant Slowpoke," Wayne said. "Next time, though, win yourself a bike that's not as old as a dinosaur."

Maryellen rang her bell five times, drowning him out. She didn't need to be reminded that she was riding her old clunker. "Just in case we get separated, we can use these to communicate. What do you say, Davy? With all that research you've been doing on communication, can you come up with some kind of bell code, like Morse code?"

Davy frowned in concentration as Maryellen fastened the bells onto their handlebars. "Okay," he said finally. "I've got it. Two rings means 'I found the station wagon.'" Davy demonstrated on his new bell. "Three rings really fast means 'I need help.'"

"Four rings means 'Officer Maryellen's bike has broken down,'" Wayne joked.

"Knock it off, Wayne," Davy snapped. "And that's an order."

"Hey, *I* give the orders, since *I'm* Sergeant Friday," Wayne retorted. "And when did *Dragnet* have *lady* detectives anyway?"

"Since I became captain!" Maryellen declared.

"Now, our goal is to find the station wagon and call the police to tell them where it is." She read off the phone number from her notes and had everyone repeat it. "I've got change in case we're near a pay phone, but one of us may have to race home to call."

"I'll do it, since I have the fastest bike," Wayne said.

"Let's split up and go around the same block in different directions. The Palms is laid out in a grid, so Angela and I can go counterclockwise. Davy, you and Wayne can go clockwise, and we'll end up meeting about the middle. If the station wagon is in our neighborhood, we should find it."

"Wow, you really thought this out," Davy said, looking impressed.

Maryellen blushed. "My dad suggested it. Since he's an architect, he notices how things are structured."

The four set out on their bikes along Palmetto. They kept separating at each adjoining block and meeting again until they'd ridden to the end of the street. Then they decided to go one block over to Hibiscus.

Lots of people were out on a sunny Sunday afternoon, so Maryellen wondered if the thieves would lay low. However, she saw lots of dogs, too, some without their owners nearby, making them perfect targets for the thieves. One dog chased them as they rode past, snapping at her wheels. Maryellen swerved to miss it and almost ran into Angela, who was staring ahead.

"Look!" Angela pointed. "A tan station wagon!" It was pulling out of a driveway and heading down Hibiscus in the opposite direction.

Maryellen stood on her pedals to pump harder. "Let's get a closer look before we ring for the boys."

They zoomed toward it. Since there were bikers and roller skaters in the street, the car didn't speed. Two boys about Beverly's age suddenly raced alongside them on their bikes, cards clacking in their spokes as their wheels turned. Maryellen shot one of them an annoyed look. She and Angela were trying to be inconspicuous!

Maryellen got close enough to the station wagon to see that the color was more green than tan and there were two little kids staring out the back window, not two dogs. When the car turned left toward town, Maryellen swerved up on the sidewalk, jumping the curb.

"False alarm," she said to Angela, who stopped beside her. Maryellen sighed. "I'm not sure we'll ever find that station wagon. Maybe the thieves know that the police are on to them. Maybe they left Daytona Beach for Fort Lauderdale."

"Isn't that good?" Angela asked. "Don't we want to get rid of the dognappers?"

"Well, it means they won't be able to steal any more dogs, but it also means they won't lead us to Scooter," Maryellen explained.

Suddenly, *ka-ching-ching, ka-ching-ching* blasted from the street ahead of them.

"Two fast rings on the bell!" Angela exclaimed.

"That means the boys found the Barkhaven station wagon!"

Maryellen turned her bike toward the road and jumped on. "Let's go!"

chapter 14
Poodle in Peril

MARYELLEN AND ANGELA raced up
the street, dodging a gang of kids playing baseball.
They took a right toward Palmetto in time to see
the backs of Davy and Wayne, who were pedaling
hard. Suddenly the two boys veered onto Maryellen's
street, traveling in the opposite direction of the
Larkins' house. Maryellen couldn't see a station
wagon, but she knew it must be ahead of the boys.

When she and Angela reached Palmetto, Davy
and Wayne were far in front of them. Maryellen
caught a glimpse of a station wagon driving slowly
as if its driver were looking for something—a dog?
She hoped the boys wouldn't get too close and
spook the people in the car. Maryellen knew the
key to finding Scooter was discovering where the

station wagon was taking the stolen dogs.

"Hurry, Angela!" Maryellen shouted over her shoulder. "We have to catch up."

When the boys veered off of Palmetto, Maryellen's heart sank. If she was guessing correctly, the thieves were headed for Highway 1. No one was allowed to ride bikes on the highway because it was too busy, and even if they could, the speed limit was faster on the highway than on the neighborhood streets, so bikes couldn't keep up.

She was right. The station wagon cruised through several more intersections in the development, and then stopped at a red light. Its right blinker was on, which cheered Maryellen up a bit. The thieves were heading south into town, not north up the coast. At least if they stayed in Daytona Beach, the police had a chance to catch them.

She and Angela caught up with Davy and Wayne, who had stopped at the last intersection before the light. Everyone was out of breath.

"We didn't want to ride any closer," Wayne gasped. "But we can see they're going into town."

"It's definitely them," Davy said. He was leaning on his handle bars, breathing hard. "I saw the Barkhaven plaque, and there was at least one dog in the back."

"Someone has to ride to my house and call the police," Maryellen said. "Me, I'm going to Bark Haven. The thieves might be headed there."

"I'll go back to your house, Maryellen," Angela said. "You three are the brave detectives. I'm the not-so-brave Angela."

Maryellen smiled at her friend. "You did great, Officer Terlizzi."

"Yeah, you did do great, for a girl," Wayne said, and then his face turned red and he suddenly fiddled with his bike brakes.

"Tell my father or mother to call Officer Polansky right away," Maryellen told Angela. "Have them tell him that the tan station wagon is going toward town, and it has at least one dog in the back."

Angela saluted. "Yes, sir, Captain!" Jumping on her bike, she rode off the way they had come.

"Are you both coming to Bark Haven with me?" Maryellen asked.

"It's Sunday, so it may be closed," Wayne said. "I'll catch up with Angela." Without another word, he rode off after her.

"Davy?" Maryellen mounted her bike. "Miss Hopkins will have to feed the dogs, even on Sunday, and if she's there, I'm going to find out what she knows."

"I'm with you, partner," Davy said.

The two sleuths headed for Sandy Lane. When they reached the road, Maryellen left Davy in the dust she was pedaling so hard.

The pickup truck was parked under a tree in front of the building, but there was no station wagon. Barks and howls came from out back as the two kids left their bikes near the truck. Before knocking on the door of the office, Maryellen peeked through the window. Miss Hopkins was kneeling on the floor removing a pink collar from a white poodle. There was a bedraggled-looking pink bow on the floor nearby.

Maryellen's mouth fell open. It had to be the missing Pinky!

"What are you looking at?" Davy whispered.

Pushing past him, she burst through the door without knocking. "That's the Palmers' poodle!" she exclaimed, pointing at the dog, who wagged its tail and tipped its head curiously. "Those thieves stole Pinky and brought her here to you. I knew it all along—you're part of the dognapping gang."

Miss Hopkins stared at Maryellen for a second before jumping up. "Dog thieves? What are you talking about?"

"The ones in the Barkhaven station wagon." Maryellen was so mad her voice quivered. "And now you're getting ready to sell Pinky to a pharmaceutical company!"

Miss Hopkins scowled at Maryellen. "I am doing no such thing. This dog is being returned to its owners."

"How do we know you're telling the truth?" Maryellen wasn't used to talking to adults this way, but she was too angry to watch her words.

"Why would I lie? And why are you kids causing so much trouble?" Miss Hopkins asked.

"Because I want to find my dog, and I think you're hiding something from us. We know there are dognappers in the area."

Davy stepped up beside Maryellen. "We think they're stealing dogs to sell to pharmaceutical companies here in Daytona Beach. Even the police are concerned," he told Miss Hopkins. "And we think *you're* involved."

"We've sent a letter to the newspaper, and soon you and Bark Haven will be exposed!" Maryellen added.

Miss Hopkins' eyes narrowed, and her face

turned bright red. She pointed to the door. "Leave, right now."

Davy tugged on Maryellen's arm. "Come on, let's go."

Reluctantly, Maryellen followed him from the building, letting the door slam behind her with a bang that set the dogs to barking again.

"Whoo-wee." Davy whistled as they walked over to their bikes. "You sure made her mad."

"That's because she is definitely hiding some-thing." Maryellen jerked her bike off the ground. "I bet as soon as we leave, she'll be off, too—to warn those thieves."

"Then let's follow her," Davy said. "We can hide at the end of Sandy Lane."

"What if she goes onto the highway?"

"We have to take the chance that she won't."

"Let's do it then. This might be our last chance to catch her in the act."

Biking up Sandy Lane, they came to a wild area of

pines and brush. They pushed their bikes deep into a thicket and, finding a clear spot, sat down to wait. They were close enough to the road to see the Bark Haven truck if it went past.

While they waited, Davy drew two tall stick men in the sand and two smaller stick men. "These are the dognappers," he said in a low voice. "This is us. We'll surround them and—"

"Shhh." Maryellen put a finger to her lips as she heard a motor rumble to life, then the crunch of tires on gravel. A minute later the Bark Haven truck flew past with Miss Hopkins behind the wheel.

"Let's go!" Maryellen pushed her bike from the brush. Fortunately, the truck was kicking up so much dust that Miss Hopkins wouldn't see them.

This time, to Maryellen's relief, the truck didn't head to the highway, but to Redbird Street, a winding back road that led toward town.

They lagged far behind the truck, but Maryellen was still able to see it turn abruptly down an asphalt drive. She and Davy pedaled to a large sign near the drive and stopped. *Daytona Pharmaceuticals,* the sign read. Could this be the lab where the thieves were selling the dogs? If so, Scooter might be here!

Pulling out her notebook, Maryellen quickly wrote down the name and address, her hand jiggling nervously. "Miss Hopkins may have led us straight to the lab where the stolen dogs are being taken!"

"We need to go back and call the police so they know where to look," Davy said.

Maryellen shook her head as she put the pad back in her pocket. "You go back. If Scooter is in there, I'm going to find him right now!" She was unsure what faced her at the end of the drive, but more sure than ever that she needed to keep going. Mounting her bike, she raced down the asphalt, her heart beating like a drum.

chapter 15

Proof Positive

SWEAT BEADED ON Maryellen's forehead
as she drew closer to a low building set back from
the road. As the pharmaceutical company came into
view, Maryellen realized how much danger she could
be riding into. If Miss Hopkins was meeting the two
thieves there, that would make three people. There
might be someone from the pharmaceutical company,
too, which would make four against one.

Maryellen glanced over her shoulder to see if
Davy was coming. She didn't want to admit that she
was afraid, but she was filled with relief when she
saw him pedaling behind her. Now at least it was
four against two.

She stopped so he could catch up with her.
"Thanks, I wasn't sure you were coming."

He grinned. "We're partners, right?"

From where the two stood they could see only the Bark Haven truck, not a station wagon. "Darn, I was hoping to catch the dognappers red-handed." Just then they saw Miss Hopkins climb from the pickup. Fortunately she didn't look in their direction. Instead she strode to the front double door and pounded loudly.

"We'd better hide." Maryellen pushed her bike off the drive to a landscaped area and left it behind a spray of fountain grass. "I'm sneaking closer," she said before Davy could warn her against it. Ducking down, she crept behind several tall plants toward the front of the building.

Maryellen waited behind the bushes, resisting the urge to scratch the spots where branches pricked her sweaty skin. Her lungs ached from the hard pedaling, and she longed to draw a few deep breaths, but she didn't want to risk giving herself away to anyone who might be within earshot. As she peered through the branches, she saw a man in a security uniform open the door and glance her way. Startled, she ducked before slowly looking up again. Miss Hopkins was talking to the man, gesturing forcefully, but Maryellen couldn't hear what she was saying. Just then Davy crept up beside her, tugged her sleeve, and pointed to a large trash container on the side of the building. There were more bushes and palms between them and the container. Could they get closer without the grown-ups seeing them?

"If we move quickly and quietly, we can hide over there," Davy whispered.

Maryellen nodded in agreement. They went one at a time, scooting behind the landscaping plants to the container. Maryellen flattened herself against its metal side, wrinkling her nose at the smell. Then she held her breath, trying to listen. Miss Hopkins' and the guard's voices were still muffled, but Maryellen could tell that Miss Hopkins was agitated. The woman's tone was shrill while the guard's was deep.

Dogs . . . labs . . . police . . . another shipment. Was Miss Hopkins warning the guard to watch out for the police?

Abruptly, the voices stopped. Maryellen peeked around the side as Miss Hopkins climbed into the truck, slammed the door, and drove off. Maryellen was confused—what had just happened? Oh, if only she'd been able to hear the conversation!

"The guard went back inside," Davy said, keeping his voice low. "What do you want to do now?"

"Look for Scooter. Obviously this place has something to do with stolen dogs."

"We're trespassing," Davy pointed out. "If we're caught snooping around, we could be in real trouble."

"I know, but we have to investigate. At least I do." Maryellen peered around the trash container toward the back of the building, which was about the size of her elementary school, with a row of narrow rectangular windows set high along the side wall. There were no cars in the parking lot out front, and none that she could see in the back. "I may never get another chance. Since it's Sunday, the place seems empty except for the guard."

"Hopefully there's only the one guard," Davy said. "I can't fight off two."

Maryellen beckoned Davy to follow her along the side of the building. They ran quickly, turned the corner, and pressed themselves against the back wall. A small car was parked by a closed door. Over their heads was a window. It was open, and Maryellen heard barking coming from inside.

Her eyes widened. There were dogs in the building, and Scooter could be one of them! "Let's see if we can get in that back entrance," Maryellen whispered.

"What are we going to do if we're caught?"

"Tell the truth—that we're looking for my dog." As they hurried toward the door, they passed several trash cans. Abruptly, Davy stopped and exclaimed, "Look at this!" One of the trash cans was heaped high with garbage, and on the top was a tangle of dog collars. "Scooter's collar is red, isn't it?" he asked. "Like this one?" He pulled a small collar from the pile and held it up.

Maryellen took the collar and studied it. "This *is* his!" she exclaimed. "See the tooth marks where Mikey chewed on it? That proves Scooter was in this building."

"Your brother chewed on a collar?" Davy asked.

"He was pretending to be a dog." Maryellen stuffed the collar into her pocket. "Now we *do* have a reason to get inside: Scooter must be here." Reaching the door, she pulled on the handle, angry when she discovered it was locked. "Darn it. There has to be another way in." She glanced back to the window behind them, and Davy nodded as if he knew what she was thinking.

When they were directly under the window, Davy linked his fingers together, making a cradle for Maryellen to step on. She put her foot on his clasped hands, and he hoisted her up high enough that she could grab the sill and steady herself. The window was propped halfway open at an angle. The glass was dirty. She wiped a circle with her fist and, craning her neck, peered inside. The room was dim, but she could see rows of metal cages stacked on top of each other.

Was there a chubby brown dachshund in one of them? "Scooter?" she called softly, and the barking grew more frantic.

"Maryellen," Davy grunted from beneath her. "The dogs are too noisy! We've got to get out of here before—"

"Hey! What are you kids doing?" The back door swung open and the guard peered around it, his narrow face set in a scowl. Maryellen startled, lost her balance, and tumbled on top of Davy. The two fell to the ground, scrambling immediately to their feet.

"You're trespassing on private property," the guard declared as he stormed toward them. He was young—not much older than Joan—but he pulled a billy club from his belt and held it in a threatening manner. "If you don't leave right now, I'm calling the cops."

"Go ahead!" Maryellen retorted. She stood her ground even though Davy was tugging on her arm and hissing, "Let's get out of here." They were so close to finding Scooter that her fear had vanished.

"Call the police," she went on boldly. "Then you can explain to them why Daytona Pharmaceuticals has stolen dogs in its building."

The guard faltered for a second. "What are you talking about?"

She held up the red collar. "I'm talking about my dog, Scooter. This is his collar, so I am guessing he's in there."

"That could be any dog's collar," the guard said. "And we don't have stolen dogs here. The head of the lab only buys dogs from licensed dealers. Now leave!" Waving the billy club, he took a menacing step closer.

"Go!" Davy grabbed Maryellen's wrist and yanked her around the side of the building. The two ran as fast as they could, jumped on their bikes, and pedaled to the end of the driveway.

"Is he coming after us?" Maryellen wheezed when she stopped to catch her breath.

Davy shook his head. "No. But I think he meant business."

"That's because he knows we're right about the stolen dogs," Maryellen asked. "I wonder if Wayne and Angela got ahold of the police. We need to tell them what we discovered. If Scooter is still inside, we're going to need help."

"Let's go to your house and find out if the police have been alerted," said Davy.

When Maryellen and Davy reached Palmetto Street, they spotted Wayne and Angela riding toward them. Davy waved one arm, and the four met in the middle of the road.

"We hunted all over for you. Didn't you hear our bike bells?" Wayne said in an annoyed voice.

"We were too busy searching for Scooter!" Maryellen said. She and Davy took turns filling the others in on all that had happened.

"So you really found Scooter?" Angela asked.

"We found his collar," Maryellen clarified, pulling it from her pocket to show them. "We need to get inside Daytona Pharmaceuticals to actually find him. What did Officer Polansky say when you called the police? Did they catch the Barkhaven station wagon?"

Wayne and Angela both looked uncomfortable. "We never got to talk to him," Wayne explained. "The policeman at the duty desk said there was a bad accident on Orange Avenue and all the officers were called to assist."

"Oh, no." Maryellen had pictured the officers rounding up the bad guys who would lead the police to the lab and Scooter.

"He said he'd make sure Officer Polansky got the information," Wayne said quickly.

"Your mom was ready to help," Angela added. "She was about to herd your brothers and sisters into the car, but we told her to wait until we found you."

"Your dad was at Joan and Jerry's, helping them fix the door on the Airstream," Wayne said.

Maryellen pounded her handlebars in frustration. "Only my mom and dad couldn't get into Daytona Pharmaceuticals either! Oh, this can*not* be another dead end. I don't want Scooter to spend one more minute in that place."

"If he's still there," Wayne said solemnly before Davy punched him in the arm to shut him up.

Only Maryellen had already heard him. She knew Wayne had simply expressed the reality. Scooter had been gone a long time, and other than the red collar, she and Davy had no proof that he actually was at Daytona Pharmaceuticals. What if the dognappers had taken Scooter to Miami or Saint Augustine? What if the lab had decided he was of no use and got rid of him? What if she never saw him again!

Maryellen's chest tightened with fear, but then she gritted her teeth. Miss Hopkins knew *something*. And that *something* was going to lead them to her dog.

chapter 16

Miss Hopkins

"I'M GOING BACK to Bark Haven," Maryellen declared.

"Again?" Wayne rolled his eyes. "Miss Hopkins isn't going to tell us anything."

"Maybe she will if we ask the right questions," Maryellen said. "Like 'why were you at Daytona Pharmaceuticals, Miss Hopkins? How did you know to go there after we told you about the stolen dogs? What connection do *you* have with the lab? And *where is my dog?*'"

Angela mounted her bike. "I'm coming with you."

"Me, too." Davy jumped on his. "She can't deny we saw her at the pharmaceutical company."

Wayne threw up his hands. "All right, all right. I'm in."

Ten minutes later they were all riding down
Sandy Lane. Maryellen was relieved to see the pickup
truck. Still, a knot twisted her insides. Wayne could
be right, again: Miss Hopkins did not have to answer
their questions.

Maryellen burst into the office, determined. Miss
Hopkins was sitting at her desk, her head in her
hands. "Miss Hopkins, we're sorry to bother you, but
we need you to be truthful this time."

Maryellen steeled herself, ready for the woman to
jump up and kick them out. Instead, Miss Hopkins
pulled a tissue from a box and blew her nose. When
she looked up, Maryellen could tell she'd been crying.

"Someone *is* using our name to steal and sell
dogs," she said as she dabbed her red eyes. "I knew
Daytona Pharmaceuticals experimented on dogs in
its labs, but they are supposed to get their dogs from
licensed dealers. We've suspected that the company
was buying dogs cheap from unlicensed dealers.
Until you kids showed up the other day, I didn't

know these dealers were posing as Bark Haven and stealing pets."

"You aren't part of the dognappers?" Maryellen asked in surprise.

Miss Hopkins shook her head vehemently. "The organization tries to find lost and stray dogs *before* they end up in labs or get hit by a car or . . ." Tears rolled down her cheeks.

Davy stepped up beside Maryellen. "Then why were you at Daytona Pharmaceuticals this afternoon? We saw you talking to that guard."

"You saw me there?" Miss Hopkins looked confused instead of guilty, Maryellen thought.

"We followed you," Davy said.

Miss Hopkins took a breath. "Well, after you told me about thieves stealing dogs and selling them to a pharmaceutical company, I knew which company it was—there's only one in the city that uses animals. I confronted the guard with what I thought was happening. I told him the police would be interested if the lab was buying stolen pets and falsely using our name. He told me to get off the property before *he* called the police."

"That's what he told us, too," Davy said.

"Why didn't you tell us your suspicions earlier or at least help us?" Maryellen asked.

"Bark Haven has been open only a year. The organization had to work hard to get the city on our side. Many people don't care about lost or stray dogs, and there aren't any laws to protect them." Miss Hopkins sighed. "The neighbors already complain that the dogs make too much noise. I thought you were snooping around, trying to help them close me down. I'm always worried the police and city will pull their support."

"What about the dogs that have been here over a month?" Maryellen asked, remembering what Mr. Bates had said. "Where do you send them?"

"We usually find homes for them, but if we can't, there's a farm in the country that works with us. The owners of the farm foster dogs that we can't adopt out."

That made sense. So far, Miss Hopkins had explained everything, Maryellen realized.

"We only accused you because we thought you were hiding something or were part of the gang of thieves," Davy said.

"Your accusations—especially your plans to write a letter to the newspaper—really scared me, so I wasn't very helpful," Miss Hopkins admitted. "If the police started getting complaints that Bark Haven was stealing dogs, they would close us down for sure. And we do such good work." Standing, she gestured to the kids to come with her through the door into the back kennel. "Come, I'll show you."

Maryellen, Davy, Wayne, and Angela followed Miss Hopkins into a short hallway that ended in another closed door. On the right side was a small room equipped with a scale and medical supplies. On the left side was a wash room.

"When you saw me before with Pinky, I was

just getting ready to give her a bath," Miss Hopkins explained. "The Palmers were coming to pick her up, and I didn't want them seeing her covered with burrs and mud."

She led them on down the hall to a room with folded towels, dog beds, cans of dog food, leashes, and bags of kibble and treats. "Supplies are mostly donated, and during the week we have volunteers to walk, feed, and clean kennels. That's another reason your accusations scared me. If donations dry up and volunteers stop coming because of bad publicity, we can't feed and care for the dogs as well as we do."

As they walked to the closed door at the end of the hall, the barking grew louder. "The dogs aren't usually this noisy, but they hear us coming. Those are barks of excitement."

Miss Hopkins opened the door, and Maryellen had to plug her ears. German shepherds, hounds, spaniels, mutts, and fuzzy dogs of all sizes jumped on the gated fencing that separated the inside kennels. Tails wagged and tongues lapped exuberantly when Angela, Wayne, and Davy hurried to greet them. The kennels were clean, with comfy beds and toys. Maryellen walked along the fence, checking again to make sure there was no pudgy dachshund. When she was certain, she knelt in front of a kennel of puppies. They were roly-poly and sleek and fell all over each other to get to her fingers.

"A man found them at the dump," Miss Hopkins said. "They'd been thrown away with the trash."

Tears pricked Maryellen's eyes. "I'm sorry I was so suspicious of Bark Haven."

"I'm sorry I didn't help from the beginning. We might have caught those thieves already." Miss Hopkins sounded angry. "Before he clammed up, the guard let slip that there might be another shipment of dogs coming late this afternoon."

"More dogs!" Maryellen stood up quickly. "We've got to stop those thieves—and we can if we work together."

Wayne, Davy, and Angela clustered around Maryellen and Miss Hopkins. "Yeah, we need to *do* something!" Wayne declared.

"There's a Daytona policeman on our side, Officer Polansky," Maryellen went on. "The city has been getting calls about missing dogs, and he's been looking into it."

"We couldn't get him this afternoon because he was at a traffic accident," Angela chimed in.

"If we can use your phone, we can try and call him again and make sure he knows what's going on," Maryellen said.

"He'll make that guard let us in to the pharmaceutical building," Davy added.

Miss Hopkins nodded. "Let's call—but if we can't get ahold of the police officer, I'm ready to confront that guard again myself."

"Only you won't be alone this time," Maryellen said, as her friends chorused, "We're coming with you!"

Maryellen dialed the police station. This time, she was able to talk to Officer Polansky.

"I called your home, but your mother said you were on a mission to catch dog thieves," he told her. "I cruised your neighborhood, but didn't find you, and I'm sorry to report that most of the officers on duty have been busy with the accident, so we haven't sighted that station wagon yet."

Maryellen filled him in on what had occurred. "Miss Hopkins thinks there will be another shipment of dogs coming to the pharmaceutical company this afternoon. We can catch them in the act."

"You mean *the police* can catch them," he said. "Thanks for the tip. We'll handle it from here."

"With our help," Maryellen murmured as she hung up, and then she said aloud to the others, "He said the police will handle it, but I want to be at Daytona Pharmaceuticals when they get there."

"Me, too." Miss Hopkins grabbed her keys from the desk. "Let's go."

They were hurrying to the pickup truck when Maryellen spotted her family's station wagon bouncing down Sandy Lane. Carolyn was waving out the open front window. Beverly, Mikey, and Tom were hanging out the back windows waving.

"Here comes the cavalry," Davy joked.

Maryellen groaned when Mrs. Larkin parked and her brothers and sisters burst from the car. Just what she *didn't* need.

"We're here to help, too," Beverly hollered as she ran up.

"We didn't want to sit around and wait any longer," Carolyn added.

Mikey cried, "Where's Scootew?"

"We're headed to Daytona Pharmaceuticals," Maryellen told her family. "Scooter might be there. We have to hurry!"

Davy and Wayne piled into the bed of the truck. Maryellen and Angela climbed in the front with Miss Hopkins, and the rest of the Larkins jumped back into the family station wagon. Sand and dust blew every-where as the two vehicles barreled down the lane.

Miss Hopkins shifted hard, yanked the wheel to the right, and stepped on the gas as she zoomed toward Redbird Street. Maryellen peered over her shoulder. She was surprised to see her mother's car right behind the truck. Usually her mom drove like a cautious turtle.

The two vehicles roared down Redbird to the Daytona Pharmaceuticals sign and turned in. Maryellen sat up on the edge of the seat. She was hoping to see a police car, but instead she saw a tan station wagon parked in front of the building. Two men stood beside it with several dogs tied with rope leashes. The guard was right beside them, taking the leashes from the guy with the scraggly beard and baseball cap.

"There they are!" she cried out. "The dognappers are here. We have to catch them!"

chapter 17

"We Want Scooter!"

MISS HOPKINS PRESSED her foot on the gas. Suddenly, the thieves looked up. When they saw the pickup barreling toward them, they dropped the rope leashes and jumped into their station wagon.

"They're going to escape!" Maryellen exclaimed as she and Angela held on to each other.

The guard scrambled to grab the whirling dogs before they ran off. He yanked them into the building and slammed the door. The Barkhaven station wagon circled, tires squealing, and drove straight toward the Bark Haven pickup.

"Hold on, girls!" Miss Hopkins hollered as she steered hard onto the grass to avoid a collision. Maryellen jounced in the seat as the pickup veered into the plantings. The tan station wagon blew past, heading directly for the Larkins' station wagon. Mrs. Larkin stopped abruptly, and the thieves swerved around her car and squealed up the drive.

Maryellen threw the door open and hopped out. Sirens blared from the far end of the drive, then grew distant, as if a police car was going down Redbird. Was Officer Polansky finally chasing after the station wagon?

Miss Hopkins jumped out of the pickup and ran with Maryellen to the front doors of the building. Miss Hopkins got there first and yanked on the door, which flew open. "It's not locked."

Inside, the foyer was tiled, cold and dark. There was no sound of barking. Maryellen looked around. There were glass-windowed offices and closed doors in every direction.

"Where did the guard go?" she cried in frustration. "We have to find out where he's taking those dogs."

Suddenly light flooded the foyer as the door opened and the Larkins, Angela, Davy, and Wayne came jostling in. For a minute, everyone stood and silently looked around. Then Davy said, "Let's each take a door. We can search faster that way."

"Just a minute," Mrs. Larkin said. "We are trespassing on private property."

"Mom, it's the only way we're going to find Scooter!" Maryellen cried.

Miss Hopkins said nothing, but she looked ready to start the search.

Mrs. Larkin hesitated, and then said, "Okay, let's go. At least we'll end up in jail together."

"Beverly, you go with Carolyn," said Maryellen. "Mikey, stay with Mom. Tom, help Davy."

"I'll stick with Angela," Wayne said.

"I'm going to find a phone to call the police again." Miss Hopkins started toward what appeared to be a reception area when the guard burst out from one of the doors.

"Don't move!" he boomed, waving his billy club menacingly.

Maryellen couldn't believe it. They'd gotten this far, and no guard was going to stop her now. "We only want to check for our pet dachshund," she said calmly.

Miss Hopkins stepped forward. "We know you took dogs just a minute ago from those thieves."

"Yeah, they're part of an order the lab manager paid for earlier," he replied.

"So you admit that Daytona Pharmaceuticals is buying stolen pets!" Maryellen said accusingly.

"That's not what I said. Those dogs aren't stolen. The lab buys them from dealers."

Maryellen pulled Scooter's red collar from her pocket. Behind her, Carolyn gasped. "What if we can prove they are stolen? This was in the trash behind the building. It belongs to our dog."

The guard stared at the collar for a second and then narrowed his eyes. "My job is to keep this build-ing secure. Now, all of you—" he jabbed the air with the billy club, "need to leave."

"We want Scootew!" Mikey blubbered as he ran forward and wrapped his arms around the man's legs.

"Hey, hey, get a-away," the guard stammered. Mrs. Larkin strode forward and pried Mikey off. The guard squared his shoulders. "Leave right now or you're all under arrest," he threatened.

"You aren't a police officer," Davy said.

"I am in *this* building," the guard snapped. "Now I've had enough of your arguing. You are all here illegally. Line up against that wall and—"

Suddenly, Mrs. Larkin peered up at the guard. "Is that you, Phil Thompson?"

"Yes," the guard said curtly.

"The Phil Thompson who was a senior in high school and friends with my daughter Joan when she was a sophomore?" Mrs. Larkin continued.

"Joan Larkin? Um, maybe." The guard looked confused.

"The same Phil Thompson who got in trouble at school because he put dead mice on the cafeteria trays at lunch?" Mrs. Larkin pressed.

The guard turned bright red. "Yes, uh, ma'am." He cleared his throat nervously. "That was me."

"I know your brother, too," Carolyn said, stepping up beside her mother. "Harold Thompson. He's in my English class."

While Carolyn was talking, her mother glanced sideways at Maryellen and then at the door the guard had come out of. Maryellen nodded. Keeping her eye on the guard, she sidled over to the door.

"Are you going to arrest the mother of your schoolmate Joan?" Mrs. Larkin asked in her sternest parent voice.

"Um . . ." The guard gulped, looking agitated. While he was staring nervously at her mother, Maryellen quietly opened the door and slipped through.

She was in a long hall with fluorescent lights that buzzed overhead. Closed doors lined both sides of the hall. Holding her breath, Maryellen walked quickly down the hallway, listening for barking. It wasn't until she reached the T at the end that she heard muffled *woofs* from a door at the end of the hall that branched off to the right.

Maryellen broke into a jog. Her heart was racing, not because she was afraid the guard would come after her, but because she was afraid of what she would find behind that closed door. Would Scooter be there? And would he be all right?

Amazingly, the door wasn't locked. She pulled it open and stepped inside a dim room that smelled like antiseptic. Her eyes adjusted to the light, and she realized it was the same room she'd peered into from the window outside. Rows of metal cages lined each wall, stacked one on top of the other. Each held a dog that began to whine and bark.

There were three dogs in a large kennel in the middle of the floor. Rope leashes hung from their necks. Maryellen figured these dogs were the ones from the station wagon that the guard had hastily brought inside before running to confront them.

Moving farther into the room, Maryellen scanned the cages for Scooter. Most of the dogs were medium-sized. Then Maryellen saw the distinctive spots of a Dalmatian in a lower cage. She knelt, and a handsome dog peered out at her. A ring of black circled his right eye. Spots! Here was definitive proof that the lab was receiving stolen dogs.

Renewed hope that she would find Scooter flooded over her. Swiftly she went from cage to cage. In the cage in the farthest corner, she spied a long, brown lump pressed against the back wall of its cage. The dog's head was turned away, and it didn't fuss and carry on like the others.

Maryellen hurried closer. "Scooter?" she whispered, but the dog didn't move. A sob rose in her throat. "Scooter?" she called louder, and slowly the dog rose to his feet. When he turned, he began wagging his tail furiously, and Maryellen knew for sure that it was her beloved dachshund.

Quickly, she unlatched the cage door and lifted him out. He smelled faintly of disinfectant, and a plastic collar around his neck read DOG No. 8.

Wiggling with joy, Scooter gave Maryellen's cheek a lick. Cradling him in her arms, Maryellen buried her head in Scooter's fur and cried with happiness. She could hardly believe she'd finally found him.

chapter 18
Dog of Honor

ABRUPTLY THE DOOR flew open, the light flickered on, and the room was filled with chattering people along with the barking dogs. "I found Scooter!" Maryellen called. Mikey, Tom, Beverly, Carolyn, and Mrs. Larkin ran over. Scooter wiggled in her arms, trying to lick each of them.

Phil Thompson elbowed his way through the group, sputtering that they were all trespassing. Everyone ignored him.

Angela hurried over, too, with Davy and Wayne. Tears reddened her eyes. "I'm so glad you found him." Even Davy and Wayne grinned happily. Then Maryellen and her friends and family joined Miss Hopkins, who was walking from cage to cage, swiftly checking on the dogs. Some of them had shaved sides or had patches taped to their skin. All wore plastic collars identifying them with a number.

"Oh, Scooter," Maryellen said sadly, "is this what they were going to do to you?"

Miss Hopkins scowled. "We've got to find a way to shut this down."

"Maryellen, look! This might be Jumper," Angela called as she pointed to a beagle in one of the lower cages.

"That's it! Everyone out!" Phil Thompson, the security guard, yelled from the middle of the room, though he didn't sound quite so fierce now. "I've called the lab manager, Mr. Showalter, and he'll be here any minute with the police."

"The police are already here." Officer Polansky strode into the lab. He looked crisp and professional in his brimmed cap and uniform.

"Thank goodness!" said the guard. "Arrest these intruders!" He pointed his billy club at Maryellen and her family. "They're trying to steal that dog."

Maryellen tightened her arms around Scooter. Mrs. Larkin was behind her, her hand on Maryellen's shoulder, and Carolyn stood beside her. There was no way they were letting their dog go.

Officer Polansky looked at Scooter, who was happily snuggled against Maryellen's chest and trying to lick Carolyn. "From the looks of it, I'd say that dachshund belongs to the family. The person the police are most interested in is Mr. Showalter, the lab manager. It seems he's been buying stolen dogs from a bunch of unscrupulous dealers from Miami."

"You caught the dognappers?" Maryellen asked.

"Red-handed. They were in such a hurry to get away in their stolen car that they forgot one dog— Mayor Donaldo's Chihuahua, Mimi. An hour ago, Mimi was swiped from the mayor's car when he ran into his office to pick up some files. We found her in the backseat when we stopped the station wagon fleeing Daytona Pharmaceuticals."

"The mayor!" Mrs. Larkin exclaimed. "So *that's*

why this gang of thieves is finally getting attention from the police."

Officer Polansky looked sheepish. "Well, that's not the only reason. There have been many persistent dog owners calling the department." He winked at Maryellen.

"Officer Polansky has been helpful from the beginning," Maryellen said. "Maybe now the rest of the police department as well as the city will feel that dognapping is a serious crime."

"And I know just who to speak to when I need more support for Bark Haven—Mayor Donaldo," Miss Hopkins said. Hands on her hips, she glanced around the room. "We have a big job ahead of us— caring for these dogs and finding their owners."

"And finding homes for the ones who don't have owners," Maryellen said.

"The Critter Rescue Club will help," Angela chimed in.

"We'll help too," said Davy and Wayne.

"Me, too. Me, too!" Mikey jumped in the air and waved his hand. Laughing, Mrs. Larkin, Carolyn, Tom, and Beverly volunteered as well.

Maryellen heaved a happy sigh. Scooter laid his head on the crook of her elbow and sighed, too. "Come on, boy, it's time to go home."

Later that night, Maryellen carried a worn-out Scooter down the hall to her bedroom. The whole Larkin family had taken the dachshund for an evening walk after he'd eaten a hearty meal of Chow-Chow kibble. Then she and Carolyn had bathed him in the tub and dried him with towels.

Maryellen laid Scooter on the end of her bed, where he buried his head in the covers and, exhausted from his ordeal and all the attention, promptly went to sleep. Maryellen sat on the bed and leafed through her notebook of clues. She was amazed at how everything she'd written down had in some way led to the capture of the thieves. Even going to Cape Canaveral had helped. (And now that Scooter was safe, she could focus on that science report and get an A.)

She was also amazed at the many sleuths who had contributed evidence that was crucial to finding Scooter. The Happy Hollisters, the Nancy Drews, the Critter Rescue Club, Miss Hopkins, Carolyn, her father, and the Dragnet team had all had a hand in cracking "The Case of the Missing Dachshund." She could not have done it by herself.

"What do you think about a 'Welcome Home and Thank You' party?" she asked Scooter as she ruffled his ears. In reply, he snored and wiggled his paws as if dreaming. She hoped he wasn't having nightmares about being dognapped.

Just as tired, Maryellen switched off her bedside light and slid under the covers. Tomorrow, she'd ask her parents about hosting a party, but somehow she knew that her mother and father and the rest of the family would be A-OK with a celebration.

The next Saturday afternoon, the Larkins' yard teemed with people—and dogs. The Palmers brought Pinky, stylish in bows. The Bateses brought Spots on his new leash. Jumper showed up with the Pursley family and promptly jumped on everyone. Angela and her parents came with Amerigo, and Buster showed up with his for-real family.

The rest of the Critter Rescue Club had been invited as well. Karen Stohlman wore her poodle skirt and Karen King a puppy hair clip. Wayne, Tom, Carolyn, and Davy paraded four dogs through the crowd. Wayne had been the first to suggest bringing some of the dogs from Bark Haven to the party. It was Davy's idea to invite neighbors who might want to adopt one, and Miss Hopkins had arrived with several rambunctious critters in tow.

The Larkins' neighbor Miss Nancy had already fallen in love with a fuzzy mutt. Mr. Brad, who had parked his truck in the driveway and was handing out ice cream, had decided that he needed a friend for his Westie—and a bigger apartment.

The dog Wayne led around, a pit bull named Boomer, had taken an instant liking to Angela's dog and wouldn't leave Amerigo's side. Maryellen nudged Davy, and the two of them smirked and rolled their eyes at the sight of Wayne and Angela giggling together over their dogs' antics.

Carolyn and Beverly passed around trays of Wheaties cereal cookies and Jell-O pops that Mom had concocted. Scooter, the "dog of honor," snoozed in a sunny spot on the front steps. Maryellen sat beside him, smiling as she watched a newspaper reporter interviewing Miss Hopkins and Officer Polansky. Maryellen was glad she hadn't mailed the letter to the editor that she and the Critter Rescue Club had written. A lot had happened since then. The reporter seemed concerned about the dog thefts, and Maryellen hoped she would get the facts straight.

The reporter had already taken a photo of Scooter

with Mikey, Tom, and Beverly, but she hadn't asked to photograph Maryellen, and that was just fine with her. This time, Maryellen didn't want her face in the newspaper or a ride in the mayor's car. She wanted the city to be on the alert for unscrupulous thieves who stole pets. Bark Haven needed the publicity that the reporter's story would provide. Hopefully, when the article came out about the good work Bark Haven was doing, they would get volunteers and donations galore.

As the reporter took a photograph of Miss Hopkins, Officer Polansky came over to Maryellen. "I wanted to let you know that the thieves are in jail and will be charged with stealing a car and dogs. The car theft will get them more prison time."

Maryellen nodded.

"Also, I wanted to let you know that Daytona Pharmaceuticals may not be prosecuted for buying stolen dogs. Mr. Showalter claims he was buying dogs from a licensed dealer. The company's lawyer isn't letting us talk to him anymore."

Just then, Mrs. and Mr. Larkin hurried over. "Maryellen, everyone wants you to make a speech," her mother said. "After all, you are the detective who cracked this case."

Maryellen shook her head. "No, everyone cracked this case and helped find Scooter. I could not have done it without all of you. Really, Mom, this isn't about me."

Her father pretended to be shocked. "Why, Maryellen Larkin, are you growing up?"

Maryellen giggled. "Not hardly."

Her mother handed her an envelope. "Maybe you don't want to talk about the investigation, but how about telling the partygoers about winning the Chow-Chow Dog Food contest?"

"We won?" Maryellen asked excitedly. She jumped off the steps, startling Scooter, who snorted awake. "The grand prize? I'm going to the Florida International Dog Show and ride around the arena with the Best of Show?"

"That's the daughter I know and love," her dad teased.

"Not the grand prize, sweetie." Her mother took the envelope and pulled out the letter. "But we won second place—a year's supply of Chow-Chow Dog Food."

Maryellen burst out laughing. That was the perfect prize—she knew just what to do with a year's supply of dog food. She whispered to her mother, who smiled and nodded.

"Come on, Scooter." Maryellen tugged on his leash. "Let's make an announcement. We'll tell the neighborhood about Bark Haven. We also need to warn everybody to keep a close eye on their pets. And then we'll present Miss Hopkins with our winnings. It won't last her a whole year, but she'll still be glad to have a good supply of free dog food."

Scooter waddled next to Maryellen as they made their way to the middle of the yard. Maryellen grinned as she picked up the dachshund and hugged him close. An expectant hush came over the crowd.

Maryellen knew exactly what to say. She didn't need to win a trip to the Florida International Dog Show. She didn't have to travel to New York City to see a Broadway show. She had the best prize in the world right here in her arms—a pudgy dachshund named Scooter.

Inside Maryellen's World

Around the time that Maryellen and her mother were dreaming up jingles to enter in contests, one real-life mom named Evelyn Ryan was doing the very same thing. She was so good at writing jingles and slogans for products that she won prize after prize—everything from appliances and food to a sports car, a fancy juke-box, and even enough money to help buy a house!

During Maryellen's time, women with children were discouraged from working outside the home, so Mrs. Ryan had few options for earning money to help support her large family. But by entering jingle contests, she was able to win enough to meet her ten children's needs and save her family from poverty. Her story, which is told in both a book and a movie called *The Prizewinner of Defiance, Ohio,* showed that with persistence—and a good imagination—it was possible to overcome big obstacles.

Several years after Maryellen's story takes place, another real-life mom named Julia Lakavage showed the same persistence in tracking down her family's beloved dog. One evening, Pepper, a gentle Dalmatian, did not return home from his post-dinner stroll. Mrs. Lakavage and her daughters hunted for days. A neighbor said he'd seen Pepper being loaded into a truck driven by a stranger, so the family drove hundreds of miles in an attempt to reclaim Pepper. But their search ended in sadness: Pepper had died after being stolen and sold for use in medical testing.

Pepper wasn't the only dog to suffer this fate. During Maryellen's time, the use of dogs in testing was becoming more common. Many new medicines and surgical techniques were being developed, and scientists tested them on animals before trying them on humans. To meet the growing need for animals, dealers gathered up strays in dog pounds, and even snatched family pets to sell to researchers. A book and animated movie about dog-napping, *101 Dalmatians*, called attention to the issue.

Later, Pepper's sad story captured the hearts of animal lovers throughout the country, who fought for laws that would put a stop to pet theft and the mistreatment of animals by the dealers who sold them. Eventually, a new law was passed making it illegal to steal animals and requiring dealers to treat test animals humanely.

The law did not make it illegal to use animals for testing, however. Today, animals are still used to test new medical treatments and other products to be sure they are safe for humans. Researchers and people concerned about animal welfare continue to debate how these animals should be treated—and whether animals should be used for testing at all.

Read more of MARYELLEN'S stories,

available from booksellers and at *americangirl.com*

* Classics *

Maryellen's classic series, now in two volumes:

Volume 1:
The One and Only

Maryellen wants to stand out—but when she draws a cartoon of her teacher, she also draws unwanted attention. Still, her drawing skills help her make a new friend—with a girl her old friends think of as an enemy!

Volume 2:
Taking Off

Maryellen's birthday party is a huge hit! Excited by her fame, she enters a science contest. But can Maryellen invent a flying machine *and* get her sister's wedding off the ground?

* Journey in Time *

Travel back in time—and spend a few days with Maryellen!

The Sky's the Limit

Step into Maryellen's world of the 1950s! Go to a sock hop, or take a road trip with the Larkin family all the way to Washington, D.C. Choose your own path through this multiple-ending story.

* Mysteries *

Enjoy a thrilling adventure with Maryellen!

The Finders-Keepers Rule

Maryellen finds a barnacle-encrusted ring buried in the sand of Daytona Beach. Will it lead her to treasure—or trouble?

A Sneak Peek at

The Finders-Keepers Rule

A Maryellen Mystery

Step into another suspenseful
mystery with Maryellen.

Maryellen amused herself by jumping from puddle to puddle as if she were Jim Hawkins trying to dodge the sinkholes in the swamp on Treasure Island. Just as she landed in one puddle, she spotted the fluted edges of a scallop shell.

"Aha!" she cried. "I found one the tourists missed!" She rinsed the sand off the shell, revealing reddish coloring along its ridges. "Beverly will love this for her shell collection."

Maryellen held the shell out to Davy, and then bent to look for more. As the sun came out, she spotted another round edge poking up from the wet sand. "This might be another good one," she said, digging under it with her fingers. But what she pulled from the sand didn't look like any shell Maryellen had ever seen. It was white and bumpy like some shells, but perfectly circular, with a hole in the middle. She swished the object through the water to rinse off the sand, then scraped her fingernail over the white crusty spots stuck to it. "I think it's a ring."

"Neato," Davy said, coming over to inspect.

Maryellen tried the ring on her pointer finger, but it was far too large. It even slipped easily off her thumb. "It'll fall off if I wear it," Maryellen said, but the words were only half out before she realized she had the perfect place to put the ring. She untied the shoelace around her neck and slid the end of the lace through the ring. It pinged against the bike key as she retied the lace.

"It's a good thing Mr. Buckley wasn't sweeping his detector through the water," Maryellen said, slipping the shoelace back over her head. "He would have found this first." Then she remembered something. "Mr. Buckley said he turned in the wedding ring he found. I wonder if I should turn this in, too."

"I don't know," Davy said. He toweled off and slipped his T-shirt back on. "That thing looks like it's been buried under the sand for ages. Whoever lost it must be long gone."

Maryellen nodded. The ring did look old, and she

thought it would be nice to keep it. She shook out her
wet hair and ran her fingers through the tangles. The
cool breeze sent goose bumps racing up and down
her arms, and she dried off as best she could. She
slipped a shirt over her wet bathing suit, trying to
warm up.

"The ring could have been lost by some tourist
from—from—Vermont!" she said, trying to imagine
a wintry location up north. "Or maybe someone lost
it ages ago while they were on a fishing trip. Maybe it
took years for it to wash up this close to shore."

"Let's show it to Joan," Davy suggested. "She
might have an idea of what you should do with it."

They ambled over to Sandy's Beach Hut. "Shhh,"
Sandy said as they approached. "It's a slow day for
customers, so I'm letting Joan study." He motioned
to a nearby spot, where Joan sat cross-legged in the
sand, her head bent over a book.

Maryellen didn't want to bother Joan, but she
really did want to ask about what she'd found. She

pulled the ring from under her collar and held it out to Sandy. "I found this in a sandbar just past the pier," she said quietly. "Do you think anyone might still be looking for it?"

Sandy looked closely at the ring. "That looks positively ancient. Maybe you've found some buried treasure."

Maryellen pictured a stash of pirate loot and felt goose bumps on her arms again, but this time it wasn't because she was cold. She looked at Sandy doubtfully. "You don't mean pirate treasure, like in *Treasure Island*?" Maryellen knew it was crazy even to imagine that, but it wasn't easy to shake the idea. "If this is what real treasure looks like, then I don't know why anyone would waste time looking for it," she declared.

"Anyway," Davy said, "who ever heard of pirate treasure buried at Daytona Beach?"